Hunting Susan

Peter Sewell

To learn more about Peter Sewell, and access FREE short stories, and excerpts from future books, please visit:

www.petersewell.com

To interact with the author and view behind the scenes video content, please visit and like Peter's author page:

www.facebook.com/peter.sewell.author

Cover design by GermanCreative on Fiverr.com

Images supplied by DepositPhotos.com

Dedication

To my children Joshua, Rebekah, Jordan, Nathan, Daniel, Caleb and Elijah. You are a source of inspiration in everything I do. I am a proud father. May your lives be filled with many years of joyful travel.
To my wife Annette, your encouragement and daily dose of laughter, means more than I can express in words. – P.S.

Hunting
Susan

CHAPTER 1

J UMPING FROM A PLANE can be frightening. Changing your identity and fleeing your home country, even more so. Susan Banks looked out the window as her plane flew towards Central America. The endless blue sky reminded her of a moment six months previously, the last time she was in a plane.

"How on earth did I let you talk me into this?" she said, raising her voice above the engine noise. Her palms were moist with sweat.

Tom leaned close and gave her an affectionate kiss. "Relax and enjoy the ride, Honey. You look cute with those goggles." He winked at Bob, the instructor. Susan had complained that the goggles didn't meet her fashion standards, but just now, it was far from her mind.

Bob laughed and stood to his feet. "Okay folks, we're at 15000 feet. It's show time!" He took the group through one last drill, and then asked the million-dollar question. "Who's going first?"

Everyone looked at each other.

"I will!"

The small group turned to Susan and cheered in support.

"Way to go, Susan," Bob said, reaching over to help her into position.

Susan looked at the fields below, then turned to Tom for encouragement. The parachuting course was his surprise gift. Not exactly the way she had planned to celebrate her 35th birthday, but she enjoyed trying new things.

"Show us how it's done, Honey."

Taking in a deep breath, Susan leapt from the plane.

"Drink for you, Madam?"

The voice snapped Susan back to reality.

"Iced water, thanks."

"Are you okay?" the hostess asked, noticing tears on Susan's face.

Susan nodded.

Reaching down into her trolley, the hostess offered her a small face cloth with the glass of water.

Susan forced a smile. "Thank you."

She looked at the small photo in her hand. Tom's blue eyes radiated with life. His straight sandy coloured hair was combed neatly to one side. This was the only picture of Tom she now had. She looked out the window in a daze. In less than twenty-four hours, her life had been turned upside down, and she was about to begin a new life in a country she had no knowledge of.

CHAPTER 2

San Jose, Costa Rica

T HE STAMP THUMPED down on Susan's passport. Her alias, Diana Smith had been approved entry. As she left the airport, the humidity welcomed her like a hot oven. She retrieved several dollars from her small handbag and approached the open window of a taxi.

"Crowne Plaza, please."

The driver greeted her with a large smile. "Welcome to San Jose, beautiful lady. Hop in."

Susan returned a shy smile.

"You're here for business?" The driver asked, while moving into the busy city traffic.

Susan turned to stare out the window. "Kind of."

He looked into his mirror and twitched his bushy eyebrows up and down.

"An extended holiday," Susan replied, smiling as she observed his eyebrows.

"A holiday. With no luggage?"

She smiled. "No luggage. No problem."

He grinned. "Pura Vida."

Susan looked at him curiously.

"It's a favourite saying here in Costa Rica," he said, looking at the rear-view mirror. "It means simple or pure life, but we also use it as a greeting, or for saying goodbye. No stress. No worries."

"Similar to hakuna matata?"

"Hakuna?" the driver said, looking confused.

"Never mind," Susan replied.

As the taxi moved closer to the city centre, her body soaked in the warmth of the sun, while her mind drifted to thoughts of her sister-in-law, Kim. The death of their husbands Tom and Alfred, had drawn them close during the past few months. Two grieving widows. Now they had been separated, each receiving a new identity and flights to Central America, without knowing where the other was. Susan studied her reflection in the window. Her once long dark hair was now short and blond. She felt drained of emotional energy, but knew she had to push on. One day at a time, she told herself.

They arrived at the hotel and Susan was welcomed by a young man at the entrance.

"Pura Vida, Senioreta!" the driver called.

She turned. "Piro Vida!"

The young greeter smiled as he led her inside. "It's Pura Vida."

"I love this country already," she replied.

****

The following day, she stopped by the reception desk. "I'm looking for a place close to the ocean, but without crowds."

"East or west coast?" the receptionist asked.

"West," she replied, without thinking.

"Tamarindo is nice. It's small and relaxing. I have a cousin living there." The man unfolded a map in front of Susan. "That's it there."

"It looks nice. I mean, I could imagine it would be a lovely place."

"You'll love it. I promise," he said, staring at the map. "I can help you book a bus ticket."

"That sounds great," she said, staring dreamily into the air.

"How long do you want to stay there?" the young man asked. He stood waiting for her response.

Susan returned to the conversion, looking into his dark eyes.

"How long do you want to stay in Tamarindo?" he repeated.

"I'll see if I like it first, then decide."

He laughed. "You seem very flexible."

"Pura Vida," she replied, grinning.

****

As the bus travelled through the countryside, Susan watched the fields of sugarcane and coffee plantations. She had only ever been out of America once before. A trip to Rio with two friends, just after leaving school. A family with two children sat a few seats in front of her, triggering her past dreams of having children and living on a farm in the Kansas Prairie where she grew up. Watching the father interact with his son brought tears to her eyes. Tom had talked about wanting children, just a few weeks before his death. Her mind replayed scenes from the past few weeks. Her brother-in-law Alfred's funeral, the news of Tom's murder, and the warning from Tom's uncle to leave the country. Only God knew how many times she had rehearsed the same depressing scenes in her mind. The two children started arguing. Susan watched them, pleased by the distraction.

After more than five hours, they finally arrived at Tamarindo. Susan walked through the centre of town, observing people, and admiring the palms and other trees. The buildings were old, but more colourful than her neighbourhood in New York.

"Senioreta!" one of the local retailers called out.

Susan responded with a nervous smile.

"You need a computer." He tapped his chest. "I'm your man."

Susan nodded. "I'll remember that," she replied.

"My name's Jose!"

"Susan!" She looked around awkwardly. "It's my first day in town."

"I can see that," he said. He pointed down the road. "You'll find a nice hotel down that way."

She nodded.

"On the corner."

"Pura Vida," she replied.

Jose laughed loudly. "Pura Vida."

Nine Months Later

Susan woke with her body covered in sweat, and struggled to slow her breathing. She raised herself and sat on the side of her bed. The nightmares had been constant during the last few months. Bodies floating face up in the water. Enlarged eyes gazing straight at her. The two police officers standing at her door. She walked to her tiny kitchen and poured a glass of water. Tears flowed down her face as she watched the silhouetted palm trees swaying outside. Sunrise was still an hour away. She dressed in her running clothes and made her way to the beach. The waves crashed against the shore with rhythmical consistency, as Susan watched the sunlight creating a trail of golden light along the beach.

As she jogged along the sand, the breeze blew hair across her face. The solitude of Tamarindo's' beach made New York seem a million miles away. Nine months ago, she was jogging through central park in Manhattan, watching old Morris feed the pigeons. Now she was alone in central America with a new name and still no idea what the future held. It was the same feeling she had after leaving school. She had experienced the same feeling of loneliness and uncertainty several times. Once after the death of her parents, once after a five-year relationship had ended, and once after leaving the Kansas countryside and moving to Manhattan.

After breakfast, Susan relaxed in her chair, listening to the children playing outside in the street. The sound of those children had been therapeutic on days when she felt too depressed to leave the apartment. She stared at the bars on the windows. In some ways, those bars were symbolic of her inner prison. A knock at the door interrupted her thoughts.

"Diana!"

Recognising the voice, Susan leapt to her feet and opened the door.

"Maria!"

Susan had met Maria during her first few weeks in Tamarindo. Maria's face radiated with joy in seeing Susan, and the two women embraced. Maria's thick black hair flowed over her shoulders. She handed Susan a bunch of flowers.

"Thank you so much. They're beautiful."

"A small gift to let you know how much we care. How are you feeling today?"

"I'm doing much better."

"That's great."

Maria took a step backward to admire Susan's dress.

"Oo la la," she said, moving her hands through the air to trace Susan's body shape. "Very sexy."

Susan smiled. She appreciated Maria's attempts to make her feel good. "I love this dress, and I have the best tailoress in Costa Rica."

Maria laughed. Susan's compliment was close to the truth. Maria was the most sought after tailoress, in the area.

"How's Anton?"

Maria's husband Anton worked for a local real estate business.

"He's well. Working hard as usual. And how are the Spanish classes?" Maria asked.

"I'm still enjoying them. It gives me an excuse to socialize and get out of the apartment."

"I'm happy for you, Diana."

"I still have good and bad days. Days when I just want to stay in bed." She looked down.

Maria remained quiet, allowing Susan to continue.

"I'm learning to forgive those who destroyed my life. It's hard, but I'm learning."

Maria hugged her again. "Come again for dinner this week. The children love having you over."

"Thanks Maria. Maybe tomorrow."

"You're always welcome. You're family." Maria hugged Susan once more before leaving.

That night, sitting in her favourite restaurant, the words of the song 'I'll stand by you', played softly in the background. She stared at the photo of Tom in her hand, and wiped tears from her cheeks. Today was Tom's birthday. Susan placed the photo on the table and removed a plane ticket from her handbag.

CHAPTER 3

Cartagena, Columbia

A S SHE LOOKED over the balcony of her hotel, Susan's blond hair danced in the gentle sea breeze. Down below, the streets of Cartagena were full of tourists. Susan had arrived several days before and was now awaiting Kim's arrival. She glanced at her watch repeatedly. The two women had planned to meet tonight, New Year's Eve. Her fingers tapped impatiently on the balcony handrail, wondering if Kim would make it.

Half an hour later, she sat outside the small café where they had arranged to meet.

"Can I get you anything?" a young waitress asked.

Susan shook her head. "No thanks."

She held her handbag nervously, while her eyes scanned the street for any sign of Kim. The girls had not been in contact since leaving America the previous year. Had Kim remembered the location? She shook the doubts from her mind and glanced at her watch again. A group of well-dressed men and women moved along the street in her direction. Susan studied the group and leapt from her chair, locked onto a familiar face in the distance.

"Susan!"

The two women ran toward each other, connecting in a hug.

"Kim, you look wonderful."

"It's so great to see you, Susan."

Susan grasped a lock of Kim's hair.

"You've grown your hair!"

Kim twirled around, allowing the bottom of her dress to fly outward.

"Very sexy," Susan said, in a voice that mimicked her friend Maria.

They both laughed.

******

Back at the hotel, the girls had changed into swimwear and sat by the pool. The sun warmed their bodies as they dangled their legs in the water.

"I was afraid you wouldn't make it," Susan said.

"I've never failed to turn up to a holiday," Kim replied, smiling.

"I'm so glad you're here."

Kim placed her hand on Susan's leg. "You've told me about your Spanish course, and Costa Rica. What are your plans now?"

Susan shook her head. "I'm still living day to day. Tom's death is something I will probably never get over."

"I know what you mean," Kim said, lowering her head.

The sound of firecrackers interrupted their sombre moment.

"Sounds like the party has started without us," Susan said, rising to her feet. "Let's go and join them on the roof."

A live band played as they stepped from the elevator onto the rooftop terrace, twenty floors high. Susan's white sleeveless, knee-length dress immediately attracted the attention of a well-dressed barman.

"Ladies, a cocktail?" he yelled, waving them over to his bar.

"Non-alcoholic for me," Kim said, approaching the bar, "Perhaps a fruit mix."

"Make it two, with pineapple, orange and cranberry juice," Susan said, "And a touch of ginger ale."

"A lady with class," the barman said, jovially.

The rooftop was decorated with balloons and filled with tables of finger food. As the clock hit midnight, the sound of fireworks, car horns and cheering, filled the streets below. Looking from the rooftop, Susan and Kim watched the reflection of exploding fireworks on the ocean.

Kim held her glass in the air. "To us."

"Strong and brave," Susan replied.

They exchanged smiles.

"To new lives, and to the loved ones who have left us beautiful memories."

Susan raised her glass in mutual support. "To happy moments, and friendship." Then she changed her tone. "And to the bitches that destroyed our families." She raised her voice over the music. "May truth and justice prevail!"

"Happy New Year ladies!"

A bearded Columbian wearing a bandana, surprised them both with a kiss on the cheek. They burst into laughter, momentarily forgetting the past, and erupting into a fit of shouting. The surge of emotions continued as they hugged and shouted to the oblivious crowds below.

****

The next morning, a knock on the door woke them. Kim wiped her eyes and sat up with a disapproving look on her face. "Who on earth is at our door at this time on New Year's Day?"

Susan staggered to the door and peered through the spy hole.

"Hotel staff," she said, opening the door.

Kim flopped back on her pillow.

"Coffee and newspaper for you, Madam," a young man with a beaming smile said, handing her a tray with two coffees.

"Thanks for the wakeup call," Susan said, rolling her eyes.

He left the room and they sat in bed drinking the coffee.

"We're up now," Susan said, leaping from her bed. "Let's start the year with a jog." She reached over and pulled Kim's arm.

"Susan!" Kim protested, grabbing her sheets.

Fifteen minutes later, as the sun shone across the waves, the two ladies jogged along the waterfront.

"You've always loved jogging, haven't you?" Kim asked.

"My father was a national hurdles champion. All my family were very sporty."

"I never knew your father was a national champion," Kim said, picking up her pace to keep up with Susan.

"I was always so proud of him growing up," Susan replied.

Kim glanced at Susan. "I'm sure he was proud of you too."

"Yes, I was always daaaaddy's liiiiittle girl." She pointed ahead. "There's a nice café near the yacht club. We can stop for breakfast there."

The girls were eating a traditional Columbian breakfast of rice, beans, eggs, and a selection of vegetables, when Susan asked Kim about the key around her neck. Kim rubbed the key between her fingers. "Two family photos and a mysterious key are all I have to remind me of the past."

"Mysterious?"

"I found it in one of Alfred's draws, with a name and address of someone in Paris."

"It looks like a key for a safety deposit box. Did Alfred have friends in Paris?"

"None that I know," Kim said. "I'm guessing it's a work contact. John Desrosiers, 67 Saint Mande, Paris."

Susan looked surprised. "You've memorized that address well."

"I've thought about the address a thousand times." Kim said, holding the key tightly.

"Maybe it's time for us to visit Paris," Susan suggested.

"Are you serious?"

"There are so many questions I'd love answers for."

Kim remained silent.

"I have forgiven those who killed Tom, but I can't live in peace until I know why."

"Susan, do you realise the risks?"

"We're taking a risk just being here. I know it could be dangerous, but I would be willing to take the risk. I need to know who killed Tom, and why."

"Tom would have wanted you to be safe." Kim reached out, touching Susan's arm. "I've fought with the same thoughts as you, wanting to know more, wanting revenge, wanting some kind of justice."

"But you must want answers too?" Susan said, grasping Kim's hand.

Kim stared at her coffee. "Alfred's death ripped my world apart. I was in denial for months, suppressing anger, bitterness, and then finally realising I was poisoning my soul. I had to release it. I had to let go." Her voice became distant. "I had to forgive; and let go of the anger." She paused to wipe her eyes. "The last eighteen months has been the most emotional time in my life. I miss my children so much, and battle with guilt for leaving them every day." She reached out to hold Susan's hand. "As much as I would like to know answers…" She slid her cup along the table and back again. "I love my life in Cuba. I've learnt Spanish, and I'm trying my best to move forward. Perhaps one day I'll get to see my children again." She wiped her eyes a second time. "What we've been through is horrible, and of course I still have questions about everything that's happened." She shook her head. "But I'm not sure I want to risk my life."

"I know how you feel Kim, and I know my faith is not as strong as yours, but during my darkest moments, I did find myself praying." Susan motioned the waiter. "I prayed many times, asking God why He allowed Tom's death." She paid the waiter and stood. "I've moved past self-pity, hatred, and bitterness toward the world. I know none of this was God's fault, and no longer blame Him, but now I wonder if perhaps God has a reason for keeping us alive."

"Right now, I'm just glad we have each other again," Kim said.

They hugged.

"It's been a wonderful morning together," Susan said.

"The start of a new year," Kim said, still wiping tears from her eyes.

"Just promise me that you'll consider a trip to Paris."

"I'll think about it," Kim said.

The next morning, Kim awoke to an empty apartment. Susan had gone for a jog alone, and let her sleep in. She walked to the balcony, looking at several yachts.

Susan entered a few minutes later, as Kim was pouring coffee.

"How was the jog?"

"Beautiful. The water is so calm. I was thinking if you like, we could go out in a boat today."

"That sounds great." Kim handed Susan a coffee and they walked to the balcony. "I was just looking at the yachts and thinking how fun it looked."

"Sounds like a plan," Susan said, raising her hand to high-five Kim. They stared at the ocean sipping their coffee.

"While I was out jogging, I stopped at an internet café."

"Oh?" Kim said, turning to look at Susan, and curious to know more.

"I googled that name."

"Name?"

"John Desrosiers."

Kim raised her eyebrows. "Really?"

"Well, I wondered how many people there were with that surname."

"And?"

"Four people. None of them lived at 67 Saint Mande, but it did match a bank."

"It was a bank address?"

Susan nodded. "It's the address for LCL Paris Bel Air. 67 Avenue de Saint Mande."

"Perhaps one of those four French men has a matching key to a safety deposit box at that bank," Kim said, pausing to stare at the ocean.

"When can we go?" she finally asked.

Susan removed her sunglasses, surprised by Kim's response. "Why the change of mind?"

Kim turned her head toward the ocean, deep in thought. "I had a strange dream last night."

"And?" Susan turned to face Kim.

"I saw a puppet." Kim shook her head. "It was a silly dream, but it made me feel confident that everything would be okay." Kim smiled. "So, when are we flying?"

"Not so fast," Susan said. "We'll have to plan our arrival and departure carefully, to avoid anyone who might be looking for us."

CHAPTER 4

Paris, France

THAT WAS A LITTLE more relaxing than our boat ride," Kim said, as their plane landed in Paris.

Susan let her tongue hang from the side her mouth. "Don't mention that boat ride …ever …again."

As their taxi made its slow journey into the city, both ladies, exhausted from travel, closed their eyes. "I never did ask how you got all this money," Susan whispered.

"Cryptocurrency."

"Anonymous transfer."

Kim nodded. "Alfred had an account."

"And you kept withdrawals under your mattress?"

"No, I hid the money in my underwear draw," Kim said.

"Sounds like you've been to secret agent boot camp."

"Call me Agent Puckerlips."

Susan opened her eyes just in time to see Kim pouting her lips. She laughed loudly, causing the driver to look in his mirror with a frown. The ladies responded by covering their faces, but the hilarity of the moment caused them to burst into laughter again.

Hôtel du Continent was situated near a large park, reminding Susan of her apartment in New York. After check in, she passed the list of phone numbers to Kim.

"Try calling our four mystery men," she said, admiring the statue of an angel on a table nearby.

"Let's see how I go with my French," Kim said, sitting on the edge of one of the two beds and picking up the phone. She dialled the first number and talked for several minutes while Susan stared out the window.

"He wasn't home. I spoke to his wife, but she had never heard her husband mention an American friend."

"Who's next?" Susan asked, still staring out the window.

"Are you serious?" Kim asked, looking at Susan with her eyebrows raised and mouth twisted sideways.

Susan shook her head and laughed, realizing the joke. "I'm sorry, you caught me daydreaming," she said. "Let's try John number two."

Kim rang the next number. "This is him," she whispered, making eye contact as Susan turned. "Is it possible to meet this afternoon?" She pointed to the bench. "Pen." She wrote a street name and ended the call.

"Well?"

"He says he met Alfred two years ago. He knows who we are and wants to help, but he used the phrase 'j'ai une peur bleue'."

Susan raised her eyebrows.

"Rough translation. He feels like a scared rabbit."

"So, he'll meet with us?"

"Yes, today at three. He said we should wait at the corner of Castiglione and Mont Thabor, and he'll send a taxi to pick us up."

"Do you think we can trust him?"

Kim shrugged her shoulders. "I think so."

Two hours later, they stood in front of Le Repaire de Cartouche, a bright red restaurant on the north side of Paris. They stepped inside and cautiously looked around. The interior was an elegant baroque style, with lighting to create a cosy atmosphere. At the back of the room, an elderly gentleman read the paper.

"John?"

The man arose from his chair. "You must be Kim," he said, taking her hand. "Alfred spoke about you." He reached out his hand to Susan and smiled. His large moustache and dark eyes appealed to her. "Susan. It's a pleasure meeting you." He addressed them both. "I saw the news reports, and I was sad to hear about both Tom and Alfred." He gestured the ladies to sit and repeated the story of how he had met Alfred. As he spoke, his fingers stroked his moustache. "He was a great man. One of the greatest minds I've ever met." He stared at the ceiling, deep in thought.

Susan sat forward. "What type of projects were you and Alfred working on?"

"Military. Natural light cloaking technology." He smiled, realising the topic was foreign. "We made things invisible," he whispered, in a husky tone.

Susan raised her eyebrows. "You made things disappear?"

His face lit up with a proud smile, and he nodded. Then he looked around and stared directly into Kim and Susan's eyes.

"There's a lot of money involved in military technology, and a lot of very powerful people with agendas." He rolled his eyes back and forth between the two women. "People with the resources to bury anyone who gets in their way. Power to make people permanently disappear. You need to be very careful, and don't go digging anywhere you shouldn't."

They sat in silence, contemplating his words, then Kim placed her key on the table.

"There's a safety deposit…"

John lifted his hand, interrupting her. He reached out, taking the key. "I'll access the deposit box and have the contents delivered to your hotel, but I'm an old man… too old for war games. I just want to live peacefully without any trouble." John held his gaze on the women and stood to his feet. "You won't hear from me again."

"Do you know what's in the deposit box?" Kim asked.

John shook his head. "Alfred said it was work related, but I learned to never ask too many questions. It was a pleasure meeting you both."

Susan and Kim watched as he walked toward the door and turned.

"Do you need help with a taxi?"

"We're fine," Kim said.

"Au revoir."

They sat in silence as John exited the restaurant.

****

The next morning, as they returned from breakfast, a knock sounded at the door. Kim opened the door to find a courier with a small package.

"Mrs. Smith," he asked, allowing Kim to take the package and sign a receipt.

She sat the package on the bed.

"Mr. Derfla?" Susan said, reading the senders name. "The package is obviously from John, but who is Mr. Derfla?"

"It's Alfred spelled backwards," Kim said. "It was a private joke among his work colleagues."

The ladies sat and opened the package. Inside, there was a small flash drive with a handwritten note.

Kim read the note. "It's Alfred's handwriting." She ran her finger over the writing. "FLASHLIGHT."

"I wonder what it means?" Susan asked, grabbing her small laptop.

Kim turned the kettle on and returned as Susan attempted to open the flash drive. A password screen appeared.

"I think I know this," Kim said, leaning over and tapping the keyboard. A new window opened, showing a contents menu.

"How did you know the password?" Susan asked, looking at Kim.

"Alfred was a creature of habit. He always used my name and part of my birth date." Kim pointed to a folder midway down the menu. "Flashlight."

Susan opened the file and a screen full of faces appeared. "This is starting to get interesting," she said, scrolling down the page.

"Who are all these people?"

"I have no idea, but they're obviously very important. Perhaps if we can work out who they are, it might help answer some questions." She spent the next few minutes scrolling through the pages of faces. Every assortment of facial hair was represented, causing her to stop and laugh more than once. Suddenly, she stopped.

"Alfred and John!"

Kim stared at Alfred's face. "Alfred." Her voice was sombre.

Susan progressively opened the other files including photos, and diagrams of various military weapons.

"Rapid Laser Discharge."

"It sounds like science fiction," Kim replied.

"They could be projects that Alfred and John were working on."

Kim tried calling John again. "It's saying the number has been disconnected."

"He may have been spooked by our meeting and changed his number." Susan closed the lid of her laptop. "Not much more we can do now. We'll have to wait and consider our next move."

"Shopping?" Kim asked, changing the mood.

Susan smiled. "Why not?"

Kim grabbed lipstick from her handbag and entered the bathroom. Suddenly, an arm wrapped around her throat and a black leather glove squeezed her mouth. She struggled to break free.

CHAPTER 5

IN A BLUR OF MOTION, Kim kicked backwards, causing her attacker to lose balance.

"Susan!" she yelled.

Kim broke free and hurled herself into the bedroom, doing a forward roll across one of the beds. The masked attacker pursued, launching himself on top of her and grabbing her tightly.

Susan stood against the bedroom window in shock, then regained her composure and reached for an angelic sculpture on a nearby table. She rushed forward, swinging it hard against the man's midback. The man yelled in pain and turned abruptly to face her. Gritting his teeth, he released a menacing growl.

Kim seized the opportunity, and thrust her thumb into the attacker's eye, causing him to scream. He released Kim, spotted Susan running to the door, and ran in pursuit. He caught her at the door and swung her backward across the room. She landed on the floor and glanced at Kim, who was now cowering on the floor between the beds.

"Please, don't hurt us. Don't hurt us!" Kim cried.

The attacker produced a knife and approached Susan.

Susan jumped to her feet and moved backwards. As she reached the wall, the man's face turned to a twisted smile. His crooked teeth and brown eyes were the only body parts showing through the balaclava. Susan grabbed a can of deodorant on the bench beside her. The attacker rushed forward, but quickly turned his face and retreated as a cloud of aerosol fumes enveloped him. Still grasping the can, Susan leapt onto one of the beds, bypassing the attacker and making her way toward the door a second time. The attacker grabbed Kim, held the knife to her throat and threatened Susan.

"Come here you witch, or your friend is dead!"

Susan froze, then turned to see Kim's terrified face.

"That's right. Stay calm and no one gets hurt." He grabbed Kim's hair, forcing her to stand. Tears streamed from her face as she moaned.

"What do you want?" Susan asked, remaining still.

"You have a package. Where is it?"

Susan pointed at her handbag. Her hand was shaking.

"Get it!" the man ordered.

Susan retrieved the memory stick from her handbag and threw it toward the man. He released Kim and caught it.

"That was easy, wasn't it?" he said, holding up the flash drive. He left Kim and started walking toward Susan. Susan took a step backward, continuing to face the man, and now standing beside the minibar. As the man approached her, Susan grabbed the kettle and threw its hot liquid directly into the mans' face. He collapsed on the closest bed, screaming in pain and removing his balaclava. Susan threw the kettle at the man, recovered the flash drive from the foot of the bed, and ran after Kim.

****

In the lobby, hotel staff offered the girls comfort while security searched the building.

"C'est horrible, horrible, c'est trop horrible. We are so sorry this has happened to you," the manager muttered.

One of the staff wiped blood from Kim's arm.

Making an excuse to use the bathroom, Susan grabbed Kim's hand. "We have to leave," she whispered, "The police will ask too many questions."

They hurried toward a fire exit where they made their way up the three floors of stairs to their room. A few minutes later, they approached a tall and very thin security guard standing in front of their room.

"Sorry ladies, I have to ask you to clear this floor and wait down stairs," he said, pointing the way to the elevator.

"This is our room," Kim said, "We need our handbags."

"I'm sorry, but…"

"The police are asking for our passports."

"I have orders."

Kim and Susan stood their ground, and reluctantly the man moved aside to let them through.

"I'll give you one minute," he said, asserting his authority. "Make it fast."

The girls rushed around grabbing whatever they could fit into their handbags.

****

"My hands are still shaking," Kim said, a few minutes later, as they hurried along the sidewalk. "Do you think that was the same man who killed Alfred?"

"I have no idea," Susan said, "but I burnt his face, so he will remember us for a while."

The girls entered a nearby clothes shop, and emerged moments later wearing new dresses and scarfs. As they approached the metro station, Kim looked over her shoulder to ensure no one was following them. Her mind was still dizzy from the attack. Susan led the way through the crowds of commuters, and as they reached the platform a train arrived.

"This one," Susan said, "We can exit at Madeleine Station."

As they entered the train, a man brushed against Kim.

"Your pocket," he said, in a voice that was just loud enough to be heard above the noise of other passengers.

Kim looked around, but continued following Susan, taking a seat next to an older lady with a blue jacket. As the train moved, Kim heard a beeping sound and felt inside her pocket. She removed a tiny electronic device and a handwritten note.

"Susan, you better see this."

Susan took the note and read it. "Kim and Susan, please trust me. I can help you. I'm a friend of Alfred's." She raised her eyebrows. "What's that?" she asked, looking at the small device.

"It has a tiny screen."

Susan checked her own pockets. Suddenly, the device flashed a message on its screen. "EXIT NEXT STOP."

"If this person knows Alfred, we need to trust them," Kim said, sounding very unsure of herself and still visibly shaking.

Susan pressed her lips together. "It does worry me just a little, that the whole world seems to know where we are." The train slowed and the girls exited the train.

"What now?" Kim asked, looking at the device again.

The device beeped. "TURN RIGHT." The ladies rushed through the underground tunnel, checking the device as they reached the exit.

"LEFT." The women obeyed the instruction, and as they stepped onto the street, the device flashed another message. "BLUE CAR."

Susan nudged Kim's shoulder. "Over there." They crossed the street, checking for further messages as they reached the car.

"MOULIN ROUGE."

The girls hopped inside the car and looked at the driver inquisitively. "Moulin Rouge, Merci." The Indian driver gave a silent nod. He had a curled moustache and turban, that made him appear like an extra from a Bollywood production. The ladies sat in the back not saying a word to each other or the driver. Kim removed a tissue from her bag and wiped a spot of blood on her arm. "I'm still shaking," she said. After a few minutes she spoke to the driver. "Moulin Rouge?" The driver nodded, continuing to drive with a word until he stopped in the middle of a quiet street.

"This isn't Moulin Rouge," Kim said.

The device flashed. "EXIT NOW." They looked at each other puzzled, but stepped from the car, leaving their mysterious driver to vanish down the road. Kim checked the device for a new message. As they waited, a man wearing a brown leather jacket and beanie approached. "Follow me," he said, walking briskly past the ladies without making eye contact. They followed him around the corner and entered a five-story apartment with a dark brown door. As the door closed, the man turned to introduce himself.

"My name is Thomas."

Susan studied Thomas cautiously, as he led them up the stairway. A thin strip of neatly-cut brown hair, protruded from the back of the beanie. If he was a government agent or undercover policeman, he was definitely not stereotypical. Thomas appeared very relaxed, not straight faced like the legal people she had known in New York.

"How do you know who we are?" Kim asked.

Thomas ignored the question, opening the door and smiling at the ladies to reassure them of their safety. "You won't need the messenger again," he said, holding out his hand. Kim handed Thomas the small device. "Take a seat. It's only a small place, but I'm only here a few times a year."

"Who do you work for?" Susan asked.

Thomas smiled. "I'll make you both a drink, and then answer questions. Coffee?"

Both ladies nodded, and Thomas left the room. While he was gone, they sat in silence looking at the paintings that decorated the walls. A few minutes later, Thomas appeared with coffee.

"Do you know who the man in the hotel was?" Susan asked, receiving a cup from Thomas.

"The guy who attacked you in the hotel was a street thug working for a man named Robert Cruse."

Susan exchanged looks with Kim. "Who is Robert Cruse?"

Thomas dialled a number on his phone, and held up his finger to indicate a quick call. "One minute," he whispered. "The girls are safe in the Pyrenees" he said, looking at the ladies and pointing to a painting of the beautiful French Alps on the opposite wall. "Yes, I'll be sure to tell them." He ended the call and sat opposite Susan. "My boss is looking forward to meeting you both."

"Robert Cruse?" Susan said, drawing Thomas back on topic.

"Cruse is CIA, a rogue agent, power hungry, and he wants a monopoly of hi-tech weapons."

"He killed Alfred?" Kim asked.

Thomas stared into Kim's eyes. "Nobody killed Alfred. Alfred is too valuable."

Kim sat forward, with eyes widened. "Are you saying Alfred is alive?"

"I'm not a hundred percent sure, but I believe Cruse faked Alfred's death."

"But I saw…"

"You saw a body…."

"Why would they want to fake his death?" Susan asked. "And what about Tom?"

"Like I said, I can't be certain, but I do know that the key players all wanted Alfred alive, because he is the mastermind."

"What do you mean?"

"Well, he worked with a team, but essentially Alfred was the Einstein of the hi-tech weapons industry." Thomas stared at Kim. "The company that Alfred worked for was about to sign a deal with a Saudi arms dealer. Cruse wanted to stop the deal, so he removed their key asset, Alfred. Tom's death was…" He looked at Susan, slowing his speech. "Tom had regular contact with Alfred. Perhaps Alfred shared something with him." He paused. "I'm sorry for your loss, Susan."

Susan wiped her eyes.

"Alfred couldn't talk about his work," Kim said, breaking the silence, "It was all very secretive."

"We don't know what Alfred's most recent project was, but he specialised in stealth technology." Thomas played with his pen as he spoke. "He designed improvements for aircraft anti-stealth radar, and camera evasion. It's even believed he was developing an invisibility suit."

"Light cloaking technology," Susan said.

Thomas looked at Susan and raised his eyebrows.

"Alfred's friend John mentioned it," Susan said.

Kim wiped her eyes. "The last story Alfred told the children, was about a boy who was stung by a bee and turned invisible." Susan reached over and hugged her.

"How did the guy in the hotel find us?" Susan asked.

"Facial recognition software. They have access to street cameras and use software to match facial features to government databases." Thomas stood and reached for a small bag. "Cruse has a team of hackers that can access cameras anywhere in the world. There are very few places anyone can hide." He grabbed his beanie and wallet off a nearby shelf. "Money buys you access to anything, and the players have money. Lots of it."

"So, who do you work for?" Susan asked.

"All you need to know just now, is that I'm here to protect you. You'll meet my boss very soon." He walked to the door. "I've got to disappear for half an hour to buy us dinner. Towels are in the bathroom. Help yourself to anything you need. I won't be long." He opened the door to leave. "Don't look out any windows; and lock the door behind me."

CHAPTER 6

THE NEXT MORNING, SUSAN stood at the window peering through the curtains.

"Don't stare too long."

Susan jumped, startled by the voice.

"A sniper might be watching you," Kim said.

Susan rolled her eyes and returned to her bed. "I've never felt like so many eyes were on me."

"It's all very creepy. I wonder how many spies have slept in these beds," Kim said.

Susan threw her pillow at Kim, not appreciating her comical mood. "Enough of the spies." She sat upright and pushed the pillow behind her back. "I couldn't sleep last night. How about you?"

Kim yawned. "I lay awake thinking about Alfred, wondering if he was still alive, where he might be, or if we would ever see each other again. Wondering if we would ever be a complete family again."

Susan wiped her eyes. "I lay in bed thinking of Tom and blaming myself for getting us into this mess."

"Susan, you know that's not true," Kim replied, sitting up in bed.

"Yer, I know, I just wonder…" She left her sentence unfinished.

Kim stood and grabbed her towel. "How long do you think Thomas will keep us here?" she said, changing the topic.

"I'm not sure, but I'm starting to miss the simple comforts of Costa Rica."

"Do you still have the flash drive?" Kim asked, changing the topic.

"It's in my bag, between some panty liners."

"Panty liners?"

"I figured that no one would search through panty liners."

As Thomas walked through the door, the ladies laughed loudly.

"You girls seem rather happy today," he said, from the living room.

They entered the room, handing Thomas the small flash drive. "The thug we met in the hotel was after this."

"Thanks," Thomas said, briefly examining the memory stick.

"We were wondering how long you want to keep us here?" Kim asked.

"We'll be leaving Paris tomorrow morning."

"Where to?" Susan asked.

Thomas gave her a teasing smile. "Have you ladies been to Italy?"

****

Early the next morning, a small Peugeot moved through the darkened streets of Paris. The car's lights beamed through the light rain and fog. Kim rested her head on the front passenger window with a small pillow. Susan wiped the fog from the inside of her window and watched people with umbrellas walking to work. People with calendars, appointments, and busy schedules. She was once one of those people. Sometimes she missed that life. A life that seemed to have purpose. At least in that life, she knew where she belonged, and no one was chasing her.

A few hours later, the clouds cleared, making way for sunlight to enter the car.

"Buongiorno." Thomas said, turning to Kim. "We should be at the Italian border by lunch time. There's a camera in the glove box." He pointed at the beautiful French countryside. "A camera can help you focus on what's good in the world."

"Thomas, tell us more about your boss," Susan said, as Kim examined the camera.

"He's a very wealthy Saudi businessman who owns several oil companies and half of Morocco." He laughed. "Okay, maybe not half."

"Why is he interested in helping us?" Kim asked.

"I've mentioned Cruse."

"The evil guy who wants to take over the world."

"That's him." Thomas laughed, amused at the way Kim had summarized Cruse's character.

"In simple terms, Cruse wants a greater influence in the Middle East. To achieve that, he's been negotiating with rebel groups. If Cruse arms the rebel groups with the latest technology, it would be bad for everyone. Perhaps hundreds of thousands of people would die in the following conflict. It would be worse than anything we've already seen in Iraq and Syria. You can say that my boss, Mr. Ahmad, is not a friend of Cruse."

"What about us?"

"My boss monitors Cruse's activities very closely." Thomas paused, changing the topic. "What do you think of the mountains?"

Kim adjusted the camera lens and took a picture. "Breathtaking!"

"We're close to the Italian border. I have a house in the mountains we can stay tonight. Tomorrow we fly to Morocco."

"How long is the flight?" Kim asked.

"Morocco is only a three-hour flight, but it's a few hours' drive to Milan where our plane is waiting. If all goes to plan, we should arrive at the palace in time for the evening meal."

"The palace?"

Thomas laughed. "It will probably be more spacious than what you're used to in Cuba."

CHAPTER 7

Casablanca, Morocco

A LARGE AFRICAN MAN welcomed them as they approached the palace gates.

"Welcome home, Thomas," he said, in a loud deep voice.

"Thanks, Bade." Thomas looked into the back seat. "These are our guests, Susan and Kim."

Bade looked through the window of the white four-wheeled drive and greeted the ladies with a large smile. "Welcome to our house ladies. My name is Bbwaddene. I hope you enjoy your stay." He signalled the young man in the guardhouse and the large gates slid open.

Thomas waved as they drove through. "His name means 'like a large dog', but he's got a heart of gold, and he's as tame as a kitten." He glanced at Susan and Kim. "Just don't tell him I said that."

As they reached the front entrance, Kim and Susan looked back and forth at each other in amazement. "This place is incredible. Look at the balcony!" Kim said.

At the entrance, Susan felt the smoothness of the marble pillar beside her.

"I'll see you ladies at the evening meal," Thomas said. "In the meantime, Leila and the other staff will take good care of you."

Both ladies gave him a parting hug, and they were greeted by three servants who ushered them into the foyer. A six-metre-high waterfall dominated the interior and the smell of water droplets filtered through the room. The women relaxed on a lounge inside the entrance, pointing to various objects around the room. One of the servants, who had greeted them on arrival, appeared from a doorway carrying a large plate of refreshments.

"Mr. Ahmad will be with you shortly," he said.

Kim and Susan sat eating the various snacks, mesmerized by their ambient surroundings. "I could learn to enjoy this lifestyle," Kim said, reaching for a piece of melon from the large platter.

"Don't eat too much," Susan said, "I have a feeling this is just the beginning."

A minute later, a young lady approached them. "Hello ladies, my name is Lily. Mr. Ahmad is ready to see you now," she said, motioning Kim and Susan to follow her. They walked around the towering waterfall, and up a large staircase that spiralled around and led to a wide hallway. Their eyes were flooded with beauty from every direction. Kim pointed to a large painting of the New York skyline.

"I love it!" Susan said, with the excitement of a small child.

Lily stopped at a large doorway, directing the ladies into a room with large folding doors that opened onto a balcony. "Please wait here," she said, pointing to a beautiful velvet couch. "Can I get you anything to drink?"

"Do you have Dr. Pepper?" Kim asked.

"Of course, Ma'am. We have many American guests." She looked at Susan. "And for you Ma'am?"

"I'll have a fruit punch."

"What would you like in it?"

"Pineapple, orange, cranberry, and a touch of ginger ale."

"I'll be back in just a minute."

Lily left the room and Kim and Susan walked over to the balcony which overlooked magnificent gardens. The sun was beginning to set, casting mystical shadows over the land.

"This is so beautiful," Kim said.

Susan laughed. "That's the fiftieth time you've used that word."

"Yes! It's Beautiful!" Kim said, taunting Susan.

"There must be at least one hundred acres of gardens here."

A deep voice interrupted them from behind. "One hundred and twenty acres, to be exact." The ladies turned and Mr. Ahmad greeted the women with his exceptionally large smile, revealing a gold cap on one of his teeth. "I'm sorry to startle you. My name is Raheem. You must be Susan," he said, looking into her eyes with a captivating smile. "And Kim, it's a pleasure to have you both staying with us." He pointed to a velvet lounge covered with beautiful cushions. "Please ladies, take a seat." Mr. Ahmad had a very relaxing quality about him. Though he was not shy in flaunting his wealth, he was able to make his guests feel like they were old friends.

Kim felt one of the cushions with gold leaf embroidery. "You have a beautiful house."

"I'm glad you like it."

They sat around a large coffee table. The base of the table was like a large glass ball with both its bottom and top cut flat.

"The base is quartz crystal. One and a half metres wide," Raheem said, anticipating the question on Susan's face.

Susan ran her hand along the smooth surface. "It's the most beautiful table I've ever seen."

"The top is Malachite. It's the largest of its kind in the world." Raheem said, with great pride.

"Thank you for your hospitality," Kim said. "It's been a stressful week for us."

Susan nodded in agreement. "We are both really appreciative of your help and for opening your home to us." Lily returned with drinks and served the ladies.

"I'm sure you ladies will feel at home here," Raheem said, "You're safe here, and welcome to stay as long as you wish."

Susan and Kim exchanged looks. "Thank you so much."

"If there is anything special you need, Lily will gladly assist you." He pointed to the plaster on Kim's arm. "How is the injury?"

"It's just a scratch."

"I'm sorry you experienced that unpleasant incident. Thomas told me what happened." He took a sip of his drink and closed his eyes in contemplation. A minute later he opened them. "Would you ladies like to hear about a dream I had?" His face tilted down conveying the importance of his question.

Kim moved forward in the lounge chair. "Please tell us."

He looked at Kim. "I had a dream about a marionette."

"A puppet?" Kim said, raising her eyebrows.

"Yes. A puppet." He held his glass on the table. "I saw myself holding a pair of scissors and cutting the puppets' strings. I couldn't see the puppeteer. It was like he was invisible."

"Mr. Ahmad…"

Raheem raised his hand, interrupting Kim. His huge gold ring sparkled as it caught the light. "Please call me, Raheem."

Kim smiled. "While we were in Columbia, I also dreamed of a puppet."

"Extraordinary!" Raheem said, his eyes lighting up with interest.

"The puppet had my husband Alfred's face, and I was pulling at the strings to free him but they wouldn't break."

Raheem leaned forward, deep in thought. Susan looked on in silence, unsure of how to respond. She had never placed any significance in dreams, yet she was curious.

"Raheem; if Alfred is alive, are you able to help us find him?"

Raheem stared into Kim's eyes. "I'll do my best."

The ladies looked at each other.

Kim's mind was whirling with thoughts. "Do you really think Alfred is alive?" Kim asked, creasing her forehead.

"I don't know Kim. I really don't know, but I'll do whatever I can to find out."

Susan sat observing Raheem. Seldom had she admired someone with wealth. In her legal career, she had encountered many wealthy people, and found most to be arrogant and self-centred, with no sense of compassion. Raheem was different. Despite being extremely rich, he had a warm disposition and displayed more human feelings than she was used to in her former life back in New York.

"I need to attend to a few things," Raheem said, as the ladies finished their drinks. "Leila will escort you to your rooms and I'll see you both at the evening meal." He bowed before leaving.

A few minutes later, Leila entered. "Hello ladies, I'm Leila." Her dark curly hair rested on her shoulders. Come with me and I'll show you the rooms." She led them along the hallway and stopped in front of a large wooden door with floral designs carved into the surface. Leila opened the door, standing back to allow Kim and Susan to enter. "This is your room, Susan."

Susan's mouth dropped. "Oh, my goodness!"

Both ladies couldn't resist kneeling to feel the thick carpet. Leila followed the ladies in and did a quick spot check. Susan rose and her eyes fixed upon a large aquarium protruding from the wall opposite the bed. The walls of the room danced with shadows of rippling water. Schools of colourful fish filled the tank.

"This is one of my favourite rooms," Leila said. "I love fish."

The ladies admired the surrounding décor. In each corner of the room were large vases made of jasper.

"That painting reminds me of where I grew up," Susan said, as she stared at a two-metre-wide picture on the opposite wall.

Leila laughed. "We heard that you had grown up in Kansas. The painting is…"

"Cimarron Valley," Susan said, interrupting her. "It's where we often went for family holidays. I love the prairie flowers in the foreground."

Leila grabbed Kim's arm. "I have a special surprise for you too, Kim."

"It feels like a fairy-tale land," Susan said.

Kim laughed. "The only thing missing is a white rabbit."

"You'd like a white rabbit?" Leila asked, not understanding Kim's fairy-tale reference.

Kim shook her head and laughed. "No, that's not necessary."

Leila took the ladies into the opposite room. The room was decorated with flowering orchids. A pair of large doors opened onto a balcony that faced toward the gardens. A large Macaw flew onto a perch surprising Kim.

"He's friendly," Leila said, walking through the room to make sure everything was in order. "You'll find some nuts and berries for him in the pots."

Kim opened the lid and took some berries. "My children always wanted to own a Macaw," she said. "This is a wonderful surprise, Leila." She held the berries toward the parrot.

"His name is Raja," Leila said. She watched Kim feeding the parrot and then excused herself. "I'll see you ladies later for dinner."

****

That evening the ladies met in the large dining hall. The dining hall featured a large chandelier that immediately captured their attention. They walked through the room admiring the design, a mixture of roman and Middle Eastern influence. A large silver plate was fastened to one of the walls, with the words CARPE DIEM inscribed around the edge.

"Seize the day," Kim said, translating the Latin.

Susan tapped Kim's shoulder. At the far side of the dining area was an impressive tapestry that covered a three-metre section of the wall. "My aunt would love this," she said.

Kim pointed to the centre. "What do you think that is?"

"It looks like a gold ring, but it doesn't seem to fit the rest of the picture. A bit out of place," Susan replied.

Lily appeared and showed Kim and Susan their places at the table. "Mr. Ahmad will be with you shortly. Can I get you ladies a drink?" The ladies made their requests, and several minutes later, Raheem and Thomas entered. Susan and Kim stood to welcome them.

"Ladies, you both look beautiful." Raheem's beaming smile spread warmth through the room. "I see my staff have been looking after you," he said, looking over their matching dresses.

"Yes, thank you so much. We were quite light on luggage, and these dresses are exquisite," Susan said, running her hand over the diamond studs on the front of her dress.

"Great to see you again, Thomas," Kim said.

"Are your rooms comfortable?" He asked.

"Yes, they're very beautiful, and no, we don't want to leave." Susan and Kim laughed.

"Relax ladies, I have no plans to take you anywhere."

As they took their seats, a parade of servants entered the room, filling the table with an assortment of food. A large portion of lamb took prime position on the table. There was also a huge fish surrounded by a variety of vegetables, and bowls of spices. After the servants had filled their plates, Raheem recited a popular Arabic blessing.

"Enjoy your meal ladies."

"I've never seen such an exquisite feast," Susan said.

"Please tell us about your lives in America."

Susan wiped her mouth with a napkin. "I was working with a law firm. My husband Tom was in the construction industry."

"I'm sorry for your loss," Raheem said, in a sympathetic tone that warmed Susan's heart.

"He was a good man. We were only married two years."

Raheem sensed the sadness in Susan's voice. "You grew up in Kansas?"

Susan nodded.

"Please tell us about the prairies," he said, widening his eyes.

"The prairie is so beautiful, especially in the spring with all the flowers. I loved the beautiful painting in my room. Thank you."

"You're most welcome," he replied.

"In the spring holidays my family often visited the Cimarron Valley." Susan stared into Raheem's deep black eyes. "In the spring there are flowers everywhere, as far as the eye can see. Just like the painting."

"I would very much love to visit that place," Raheem said. "I was once in the desert just after it had rained, and the whole desert came to life. All the different coloured flowers were suddenly in bloom." He looked at Susan. "It was one of the most beautiful things I have ever witnessed."

A few minutes later, Kim pointed to the far wall. "What is the gold ring in the tapestry?" She asked.

Raheem leaned forward. "It's the art of distraction." He looked down at his own gold ring. "The ring captures your focus, but the real magic is happening in a very different location." He looked across at the tapestry. "Can you see the magic?" he asked, lowering his voice in a mystical way.

The ladies looked at the picture and Kim gasped. "Oh, my goodness. I see an old man," she said, excited by her discovery.

Susan continued examining the tapestry. "I only see trees and a small pond," she said.

Kim pointed toward the tapestry. "It's an optical illusion. Look above the pond and you'll see a mouth shape."

Susan continued to stare until she was suddenly aware of an old man's face. "He looks like a pirate."

Raheem laughed. "I have always loved illusions since I was a small child." His eyes glanced at a servant, who rushed to fill his glass. "I still remember the first magic show I saw. I was just five years old. My father took me to the show for my birthday." Kim placed more vegetables on the side of her plate.

"I remember sitting in the front row and watching as the magician made doves appear from thin air."

"What was your mother like?" Kim asked, changing the topic.

Raheem leaned back into his chair. "My mother died when I was just two years old, so my aunt came and looked after us." He smiled. "My mother made this tapestry." He connected with the tapestry in a gaze of silence. "It's the only thing I have to remind me of her."

"It must have been hard without a mother."

"It's hard for anyone to be without a parent, but I'm fortunate to have had such a wonderful aunt in my life."

"What about marriage?" Susan asked.

Raheem turned to face Susan.

"I hope we're not asking too many questions."

"No. I love talking about my family," he replied. A servant placed more food on his plate. "I was married for twenty-three years. My wife's name was Esther. She was a wonderful woman."

"What happened?"

"She became ill and we lost her." He lifted a napkin to cover his mouth.

"I'm sorry," Susan said.

"I've been alone now for several years; but not lonely." He looked around the room. "My wife organised the building of this palace. She was an organised woman, and extremely talented in interior design."

"Your wife did a wonderful job," Kim said.

"Yes, she worked tirelessly; helping with every detail."

They continued eating the meal in silence, then Raheem turned toward Leila and said, "It's a beautiful night outside. Perhaps we could enjoy dessert on the balcony." Leila nodded.

"That sounds lovely," Kim said.

"Kim, tell us about your life. Where did you grow up?"

"I grew up in Chicago, where I met Alfred. We attended the same college. My parents owned a small grocery store. I loved the store. My parents taught me to serve customers, and later I was able to manage the shop when they were away." She paused. "I still miss the snow at Christmas time."

"I also enjoy the snow very much," Raheem said. "Every winter I love to go skiing in Switzerland."

"Alfred and I loved to ski as well."

"Tell us about your children."

Susan looked sympathetically toward Kim, and watched as tears formed in her eyes.

"We have two boys," she said. "Samuel will be 14 this year, and Aaron 12." She paused to wipe her eyes.

"Hebrew names," Raheem said.

Kim looked around the table. "Those names meant a lot to us. Kim paused. "Our son is a born leader. He won many awards at school and was the captain of his baseball team." She stopped to wipe more tears from her eyes, and Susan reached around her shoulders.

Thomas broke the silence. "Thank you for sharing with us, Kim. We all realise how hard it must have been for you the last two years."

Kim nodded, wiping her face.

"And your other son, Aaron, what is he like?" Raheem asked. His eyebrows lowered to express sympathy.

"Aaron is different to his brother. Not sporty at all. He's a thinker. He was Orlando's junior Chess champion. We were so proud of both our boys." She paused to wipe more tears. "Sorry. I haven't had the opportunity to share like this for a long time."

They finished the meal and followed Raheem outside to the balcony. The gardens had become a silhouette in the stillness of the night.

"I've been thinking of our dreams this afternoon," Raheem said, interrupting the silence. "We'll have lots of time to talk about this again tomorrow, but I wanted to personally thank you ladies for trusting me. I realise a lot has happened, and you don't really know me."

"Thank you for making us feel at home," Kim said.

"Here in Casablanca, you can feel safe to come and go whenever you like," Raheem said. "I'll introduce you to my security personnel tomorrow, and whenever you like, they can escort you around town." He beckoned one of the servants waiting in the doorway. "Please let my staff know if there is anything you need. They have been instructed to treat you as family."

CHAPTER 8

"I SEE YOU HAVE been enjoying our gardens," Thomas said, meeting Kim and Susan at a large fountain, which was visible from every part of the property.

"The garden is wonderful!" Susan said, touching the leaf of an exotic palm. "The plants are incredible."

"We fly in experts from…" The loud call of a peacock interrupted him. Thomas laughed. "That's the call for lunch."

He led the ladies through the gardens to a roman-styled courtyard and swimming area. The courtyard was surrounded by tall palm trees with a latticed roof stretching over an eating area. The ladies sat in a lounge chair, while Thomas walked to the edge of the pool to remove a submerged leaf.

"It's been a relaxing day," Kim said.

Susan lay her head back. "I'm happy to stay here a few years."

Thomas laughed. "I think Raheem likes you, Susan."

She glanced at Kim. "I think any woman could happily fall in love with a man as rich and caring as Raheem." Romance was far from Susan's mind as she left Costa Rica, but meeting Raheem, had stirred her emotions in a way she never expected.

Lily led a parade of servants carrying large silver food platters. The abundance of food was now becoming a familiar sight to the women. Lily greeted them. "Mr. Ahmad will be joining you in a few minutes." She placed a large plate of fruit on the table.

Kim gave Susan a teasing look. "We are all excited to see Mr. Ahmad again, aren't we Susan?"

Susan bit the side of her lip, and narrowed her eyes at Kim, not appreciating the attention.

"Please begin eating," Lily said, bowing politely.

As Raheem joined them at the table, the peacock displayed its feathers nearby. "I hope you ladies have enjoyed your day."

"Yes, thank you. You have a wonderful garden," Kim said.

Susan sat silent, as Raheem stared across the table.

"I have the information you asked for," Thomas said, removing a folded document from his pocket and placing it on the table.

Raheem skimmed its contents and looked at the ladies. "We have a small team working on a surprise for Cruse. Thomas will leave on Thursday." The ladies looked at Thomas.

"Nothing dangerous I hope," Kim said, showing a concerned look.

"Everything involves some risk, but preparation helps us to manage the risk," Thomas replied.

****

That night, Kim turned restlessly under the sheets. Even the luxurious palace beds weren't helping her sleep. She rose from her bed and silently walked down the hallway. After finding an entrance to the large balcony, she walked outside. The smell of jasmine flowers filled the air. She stared into the sky listening to the sound of insects serenading each other.

"You can't sleep either?"

Kim jumped.

"I'm sorry for startling you."

Kim recognised Raheem's gentle voice.

"I often come here when I can't sleep," he said.

"There is something special about the solitude of night," Kim replied, "Especially looking at the stars."

Raheem stepped forward to stand beside her. I also enjoy watching the stars. I see the stars and try to imagine the hundreds of great men throughout history; who have also looked into the heavens," Raheem paused. "I imagine the prayers they might have prayed. How they might have felt before making important decisions or entering a battle. I try to imagine how they would respond to conflict and injustice in the world." He looked at Kim, who nodded in agreement. "Somehow it's reassuring to know that you're not alone. To know that others have been through similar situations."

"Yes, your right," Kim said. "When I feel fragile and helpless, I try and remember that God is watching over me."

They both gazed at the stars without a word until Raheem finally dismissed himself. "It's been lovely talking to you, Kim."

He turned to leave, then stopped. "We all need reminding that there is someone greater watching over us."

Kim didn't realise how valuable those words would soon be.

CHAPTER 9

Delta Bunker, Nevada Desert

WE HAVE NEW INTEL on Susan Banks," Scott said. He paused, awaiting a response. Scott Denman was a muscular man in his fifties, with a military haircut. He led a surveillance team with direct orders from Cruse. It was a love-hate relationship. He loved the work, but Cruse could make his life miserable, and he did everything he could to avoid that.

"Great. Where is she now?" Cruse replied.

"Saint Louis."

"Take her to Delta."

"Okay."

"What about Kim Knox?"

"Nothing on Kim Knox, but we expect she is close by," Scott replied.

"I want everyone working on this. Don't let them get away!"

Scott ended the call, relaxing into his chair and massaging his neck. The two women were an annoying lose end that was consuming too much of his team's resources.

"Scott, we just had another match on Banks. This time in Dallas."

"What the hell!" Scott moved his chair back and forth, clearly annoyed.

"Here's the image taken just now at Dallas airport," Drew said. Drew was a seasoned CIA operative. A well-built man with a five-o'clock beard. The type you might see playing college football. "The facial-recognition software gave us a perfect match." He zoomed in on the image, which displayed on a large wall monitor.

"How on earth does someone get from Saint Louis to Dallas, in less than twenty minutes?"

Drew looked at Scott with a blank face, then shrugged his shoulders.

"We have another one."

Scott jumped from his seat and stepped toward the digital map that filled the wall in front of him. The map registered facial matches across the country. "I want this equipment checked!" Scott yelled, pacing back and forward. "And if there's a hacker in the system, I want a bulldozer through his house this afternoon!" He left the room yelling profanities.

The rest of the team stared in Drew's direction. As assistant team leader, he was the one that kept everyone on task after Scott's meltdowns. Twenty minutes later, Scott re-entered the room. "I want Susan Banks in this building by tomorrow, and I don't care if we have to fill this place with every look-a-like." His voice was filled with determination. "How many matches do we have now?"

"Almost 70," Drew replied.

"This is going to take longer than I thought. Okay, listen up…"

"Sir, we have an interesting development," a young man said, raising his arm to get attention.

"What is it now?" Scott asked, annoyed by the interruption.

"It appears that all the Banks look-a-likes are booking flights to New York."

Everyone in the room exchanged glances.

"What on earth is going on?" Scott said, his voice fading. "Stay on it, and I want a minute by minute update." He gripped the back of his chair to mask any tension. "And I want Susan Banks in front of me by tomorrow." He stared directly at every face to reinforce his point. "This whole thing is a…" He shook his head, to keep from swearing. There was already enough tension in the room. Cruse would be calling back in a few hours and they still didn't have any solid leads on Susan Banks' location.

Club 500, Central Manhattan

As ladies gathered on the footpath waiting for the doors to open, the atmosphere was filled with laughter, excitement and curiosity. Each of the ladies wore a latex mask in the likeness of Susan's face. It was the first time any of them had met. Tourists stopped to take pictures, as the ladies posed together. Nearby, a TV camera crew was setting up to film the gathering.

Inside the recently renovated club, a large glitter ball hung prominently in the middle of the room. Soft coloured lighting helped create a relaxing ambience, while Thomas prepared his team for the grand entrance of guests.

"Okay everyone. It's 6pm. Let's give the ladies a royal welcome!" he said.

A large African man, dressed in an immaculate suit, called to the crowd. "Attention ladies! We are about to open the doors. Please have your tags clearly visible as you enter."

Suddenly, the doors opened, and after scanning their stylish ID tag which hung on a gold chain around their neck, each lady was ushered inside. As the procession of masked ladies entered, they were greeted by attendants with platters of food and drinks. The room slowly filled with laughter and conversation.

"That's 470 ladies registered," one of the attendants said, as she passed by Thomas.

Thomas nodded and stepped onto a small stage in front of a microphone. "Gooood eveniiiiiing laaaadies!" he said, dramatizing each word. "It's great to have you all here tonight. We want you to enjoy the evening, and we have lots of wonderful surprises planned." He was interrupted by loud applause and cheering. "We're expecting the last of our guests in about 20 minutes. In the meantime, let the party begin!"

A DJ took his position and the room filled with the sound of a rhythmic dance beat. A cloud of glitter fell from the ceiling, causing the room to erupt with a loud cheer and spontaneous dancing.

"Thomas, we have a reporter asking for you," one of the staff said, pointing at the door. Thomas met the reporter outside and introduced himself.

"We're wondering if you can tell us what's happening here," the reporter asked, holding a microphone toward Thomas. "Are you a member of Susan Banks' family?"

"I am a friend of Susan," Thomas replied.

"And can you tell us the purpose of this event?"

"We are here tonight to highlight the suspicious circumstances in which Susan disappeared, and draw attention to the fact that there has never been a full investigation, even though Susan was being kept in police protection shortly before her disappearance. Today also marks exactly two years since Alfred Knox's death."

"Who do you hold responsible for her disappearance?"

"I'm not here to speculate. All we want is the authorities to do their jobs." Thomas smiled at the camera. "Please excuse me. I think all our guests have now arrived."

Observing everything from a van parked across the road, Scott prepared his men. "Okay boys, it's time to move."

"And the damn media?" Drew asked.

Scott laughed. "That's our guys. Tell Thomson to block the streets."

Dressed in full offensive gear and guns drawn, Scott's team appeared from the back of the van and rushed into the club. The club filled with high pitched screams. Then just as quickly the mood changed, and one by one the women clapped.

One of the women climbed a stool. "The men are in the house!" A loud cheer echoed through the room and glitter rained down upon Scott and his team.

Scott stood speechless, regained his composure, and then yelled at the top of his voice. "Where is Thomas Lansdowne!"

His men forced the crowd backwards, yelling and waving their guns.

"And off with the masks!" he yelled.

The music stopped, and unsure of what was happening, the women complied. As the masks came off, the appearance of the room changed and each lady revealed her true identity.

Scott's men began questioning everyone. They all told a similar story. Each had received cash for what they believed was an amateur acting role. Though they searched the club thoroughly, Thomas had disappeared.

On the other side of the world, Kim and Susan watched the events from within Raheem's private cinema.

"What on earth just happened?" Kim asked.

Raheem laughed. "Cruse is so predictable."

"Where is Thomas?" Susan asked, "Is he okay?"

"Thomas is fine," Raheem said. "He planned his exit several months ago."

"But how did he disappear?" Kim asked, growing curious.

"These guys," he said, pointing to the screen, "They're all trained to look for the same thing. They are looking for a secret door, a hole in the roof, or something hidden under a mat." Raheem smiled, realising that he sounded vague. "If I disappeared from this room, where would you look?"

Susan studied the room. "First, I would look under the chairs. If you weren't there I would check behind the curtains." She pointed to thick purple curtains each side of the cinema screen.

"Most people would do the same." Raheem rose to his feet and bowed with dramatic flair. Then he held a small remote in the air and pressed a button. The girls held their chairs as the whole cinema started rotating.

"Oh, my goodness!" Kim's mouth dropped open. "Are we moving?"

Susan laughed, as she realised what was happening. "Raheem, you are full of surprises."

Kim glanced back and forward between Raheem and Susan.

"I had the cinema made in duplicate. This remote makes it rotate," he said. "This way ladies."

They stepped through the doors and Kim and Susan looked around. "We're back where we started!"

Raheem smiled. "Would either of you like to join me for a short evening walk?" he asked.

Kim excused herself. "I might head to bed. It's after midnight and it's been a long day."

Raheem and Susan said goodnight to Kim and continued outside to the garden.

"I'm worried about Kim," Susan said, as they walked along one of the paths.

"Why do you say that?"

"Since meeting you, Kim is living with the hope of being together with Alfred, and we still aren't really sure if he's alive. What happens if Alfred isn't alive?" She paused, awaiting Raheem's response.

"God is the author of our hopes. He alone can keep a fire burning, even in the midst of a storm."

They walked in silence toward the fountain, and as they turned to make their way back to the palace, Susan touched Raheem's arm. "Do you think we can bring Cruse to justice?"

Raheem stopped to look into her eyes. "It's not our duty to serve justice, but we can do what we know is right." He continued walking. "Justice will eventually prevail, but we need to respond from a position of moral duty, and not out of revenge. Let's wait and see the outcome of our party." He excused himself and turned toward his room, stopping at the door. "Your face looked beautiful on the big screen tonight."

Susan brushed a strand of hair aside. "Thanks."

"Good night, Susan."

Susan pressed her lips together and walked down the long hallway. Only after reaching her room did she allow herself to smile openly. "I'm not falling for his charm," she said, squeezing her eyes together.

CHAPTER 10

Casablanca, Morocco

KIM AND SUSAN WERE returning from a massage the next morning, when they met Thomas.

"Great to see you made it back safely."

Thomas greeted them with a hug. "Thanks ladies. I see you're enjoying the pampered lifestyle."

"We're also falling in love with the delights of Moroccan cuisine," said Susan.

"That's great. Listen, I have a meeting with Raheem now, but I'm going sailing in an hour. If you'd like to join me, you're welcome."

"That sounds exciting. Count me in. It will be an opportunity to get out of the house."

Kim laughed at the irony of what Susan had said. "Yes, the house does get a little mundane," she said. "I don't feel like sailing though. I might just relax in the garden."

"You could get Big Ben to take you shopping."

Thomas looked puzzled. "Big Ben?"

"It's the nickname we gave one of the security guards," Susan replied.

Leila interrupted, handing them drinks. "I'll see you in an hour, Susan," Thomas said, excusing himself.

"These fruit cocktails are beautiful," Susan said.

"I'm glad you like them." She faced Kim. "While the others are sailing, we could play some piano together."

"Yes! I'd enjoy that," Kim replied.

Susan hugged Kim. "I'll see you tonight."

The ladies went their separate ways, and an hour later, Susan met Thomas in the foyer.

"Ready for some adventure?" Thomas asked.

"Yes!"

"We can take my bike."

"I'm not that adventurous," Susan said, teasing.

He laughed. "Great. The bike it is," he said, handing her a helmet. "Don't worry. I'm a safe rider."

"Hang on tight," he said, as they mounted the bike.

As they made their way to the gate, Thomas looked over his shoulder, checking that Susan was comfortable.

"I'm fine. Just watch the road," she said.

They passed by sellers displaying carpets, clothes, pottery and beautiful jewellery on the streets. Thomas slowed the bike and stopped next to a small fruit stand. "These guys sell the best mangoes," he said, remaining seated.

A young man ran toward him with a tray of delicious fruit. Thomas selected two of the fruit, and they continued toward the ocean.

****

Kim was in the middle of applying makeup when several loud gunshots interrupted her routine. She ran to the door.

"Kim!" Leila's face was white. "Hurry!" she yelled, grasping Kim's arm and running to the far end of the hallway.

Loud shouting followed them up the stairway. As the two women entered a bedroom, they scanned the room for a suitable hiding place.

Kim's eyes were frozen wide. "What's happening?"

The voices came closer as the intruders made their way up the staircase and along the hallway.

"Over here," Leila whispered, pointing to a lounge chair. She realised there was only enough room for one of them and ordered Kim to lie on the floor. She pushed Kim's body between the wall and the lounge chair, making sure her feet were concealed from view. As the men's voices grew louder, Leila ran and hid inside a cupboard. A split second later, the outer door opened and several people rushed into the room. Kim identified three different voices. Her heart raced. The cupboard door opened and Leila screamed, then Kim heard a loud slap and one of men yelling in pain. The man shouted, and then slammed the cupboard door. Kim heard four gunshots as the man continued yelling. The cupboard opened again, and Kim's body started to shake.

"Noooooo!" Leila screamed, as the men shouted threats and grabbed her.

Kim listened as the men finally left the room with Leila.

****

Meanwhile at the marina, Susan and Thomas registered their visit at the security checkpoint and made their way toward the yacht.

"That's unusual," Thomas said, as they reached the walkway leading to their boat.

"What?"

Thomas frowned. "I thought I saw a man on Denise's boat."

"Denise is a friend?"

"Yes. She's an English property investor, who loves bringing her family here for holidays. I wasn't expecting her until next month."

"Her boat is the one with the gold stripe?" Susan asked.

"Yes. Ours is the one in front," he said, pulling out his phone. "I'll try calling her."

"I just saw a head in the window," Susan said.

"Are you sure?"

"Yes, dead sure." She reached over and held Thomas's arm.

They turned around and started walking back toward the security checkpoint. As they approached the end of the walkway, the sound of gunshots exploded across the marina. They looked up as one of the security guards fell backwards and two men ran toward them. Thomas grabbed Susan and dived into the water. Half a minute later, they emerged behind one of the boats, gasping for air and listening for their attackers. Thomas pointed to a row of boats opposite. "Do you think you can make it to the other walkway?"

"Do we have a choice?" Susan whispered.

Thomas shook his head. "On the count of three; and stay under until we get to the other side of the green yacht."

As they disappeared under the water, Susan's heart beat furiously. It was impossible to see clearly, but she could follow Thomas. Their heads finally emerged behind the green yacht. They both gasped for air and held each other.

"Good job," Thomas said, encouraging Susan.

"What now?"

He held his finger up signalling Susan to remain silent. They listened to the sound of footsteps along the walkway. More gunshots were fired near the security checkpoint, and several people screamed. Thomas took Susan's hand and led her under the walkway. They remained silent, tracking the footprints above them. The man passed by, unaware of their presence.

****

Inside the palace, Kim remained in a state of shock, not daring to move. She held her eyes shut and listened for movement in the hallway. Outside the front of the palace, she could hear shouting and gunshots. After several minutes, the sound of fighting stopped. Either the security guards had fled; or been killed. The sound of Leila's voice returned along the hallway. Kim shook. As the men re-entered the room, she heard Leila crying. Suddenly, a pair of hands grabbed her legs, and she was dragged from her hiding place and into the middle of the room. She looked upward, as a large man in a camouflaged uniform pushed the nozzle of his rifle into her side. He yelled several commands and waved his arms. Kim rose and one of the men pushed her towards Leila. The two women grabbed each other in a tight embrace.

"We have the American!" One of the men shouted into a two-way radio.

A pistol was pressed against Kim's forehead. Kim squeezed her eyes together, expecting to be shot. Tears ran down her cheeks. Leila yelled something in Arabic, which helped break the tension. They were led from the room and taken outside to the rear palace courtyard. A large four-wheel drive stopped, and both women were pushed toward it. One of the men tied Kim's hands behind her back and called for Abdul, the leader. Adbul was a well-built man with a short beard, tanned skin, and a crooked nose. Undoubtedly caused by a fight he had initiated. He approached the women and pointed his gun at Leila. Kim screamed and Abdul fired his gun, purposely missing Leila. He turned and laughed at Kim, enjoying the fact that he could inflict fear at will. He returned his gun in Leila's direction and yelled in Arabic. Leila rose to her feet and took several steps backward. Abdul fired several bullets at her feet and Leila turned and ran toward the gardens. Adbul aimed his weapon squarely on her back and prepared to fire his last shot. As Leila ran, suddenly an explosion threw her to the ground. Smoke rose into the air as the palace was engulfed in flames. Distracted by the explosion, Abdul shouted a command, and his team hurried into the back of the awaiting car.

****

Back at the marina, Thomas pulled himself up onto the walkway, and offered his hand to Susan, helping her up. "I think they're gone." Susan collapsed on the walkway, and watched the attackers leave the harbour in a small speed boat.

"I hope Kim is alright," Susan said, standing to her feet and following Thomas to the bike. She admired the way that Thomas kept his cool in any situation. Less than 24 hours ago, he was confronting Cruse's gunslingers, and now he had just saved her life.

As they approached the palace gates, Thomas stopped the bike and ran to a security guard who was semiconscious. Smoke continued to fill the sky and the guard looked around dazed as medical personnel assisted him.

"What happened?" Thomas asked.

"There were too many of them." The guard's voice faded to a whisper. "They took us..."

Thomas reached out in support and touched his shoulder.

"They took us by surprise."

Thomas looked up as Susan ran toward the palace.

"Susan!"

"We have to look for Kim!" she yelled, continuing at full pace toward the palace.

Thomas met Susan in front of the palace entrance, which was surrounded by firefighters. They walked around to the back of the palace and found Leila, who was being treated by a police officer.

"What happened?" Thomas asked, bending down to place his hand on her shoulder.

Leila's face was covered in tears. "There were men with guns."

"Have you seen Raheem and Kim?" Susan asked.

Leila burst into tears. "They took Kim." She wiped her face.

"And Raheem?"

"I heard gun shots in the study room."

Thomas and Susan rose, walking toward the burning rubble. The glowing flames complimented the colours of the sky as the sun set. They passed a body on the ground, and Thomas knelt to check the pulse. "One of the servants," he said, looking back toward the flames. "There's nothing we can do here."

They circled the building a second time looking for any signs of Kim or Raheem. Their eyes stung as they peered through the smoke. "It's time to go," Thomas said, "Whoever did this, may return for us."

They stared at the fire, holding each other for mutual support.

"Where do you think they have taken Kim?" Susan asked.

"I'm not sure, but I'm going to find out."

They turned to walk away, as more emergency vehicles arrived.

"What about Leila?"

"She has friends in town."

"And Raheem?"

Thomas lowered his head. "Let's hope he managed to escape." They both stared at the building again before returning to Leila. As they approached her, Thomas reached out and she collapsed in his arms. Susan held her arm around Leila in a group embrace, and wiped tears from Leila's face.

CHAPTER 11

D O YOU THINK Cruse has Kim?" Susan asked. Thomas shook his head.

"I'm really not sure what to think," he said, his voice sounding despondent. "Cruse has the support of some serious groups in the middle east. Those men we saw at the marina today were probably part of a rebel group based in Egypt."

"How do you know that?" Susan asked.

"I recognized the accents, but at least one of the men was a local, so they have local contacts." He looked across the table at Susan. "I have a friend meeting us in half an hour."

Susan looked at Thomas with hopeful eyes. "Will he know where Kim is?"

"I'm not sure, but if Kim is still in the country, we need to move fast to find her." Thomas looked down at his watch. "We can't do much until she gets here," Thomas said.

"She?" Susan replied.

"Her name's Freda." The waiter came and sat drinks on the table. "Freda is a former prostitute. She has a family now, and works as a singer, but still has lots of interesting contacts in Casablanca." Thomas read the look on Susan's face. "My best friend married her."

"Thanks for clarifying. You are a true gentleman, Thomas."

Several minutes later, Freda arrived. Susan stared at Freda's shining black skin, huge white smile, and long curly hair. It wasn't hard to see what men would like about her.

"Thomas, you old cat. What's happenin?" Freda had an outgoing personality that made everyone feel at ease.

"Freda, this is my friend, Susan."

Freda reached out to greet Susan with a hug. "It's a pleasure to meet you Susan."

Thomas got straight to the point. "A friend of ours was kidnapped this morning."

Freda's eyebrows furrowed. "That's horrible. Any idea who was involved?"

"Possibly an Egyptian group with local connections."

Freda reached out to hold Susan's hand. "I'm really sad about your friend."

"Do you know anyone who might be able to help us?" Thomas asked.

"What does Raheem say?"

"Raheem is missing. The palace is completely destroyed."

Freda held both cheeks. "No way!"

"Do you have any information that could help us?" Thomas asked.

Freda leaned her body closer to Thomas. "A group of Egyptian men have been staying in Sidi Bernoussi." She stared at Thomas. "But you're gonna need help to get close to them."

"Any ideas?"

"I know a few of the girls who work that area. Maybe one of them knows something."

"That's great."

Freda looked at Susan. "I can't make any promises. Your friend might already be out of the country." Her eyes connected with Susan for what seemed eternity, before turning away. "I'll make some calls and get back to you."

Thomas nodded his approval.

"So sorry to hear about Raheem." Freda wiped her eyes and stood, preparing to leave. "Raheem is missing," she repeated. "Derek will be devastated. He was a good friend of Raheem's."

"I'll call you later," Thomas said.

"Thank you for your help, Freda," Susan said, standing to embrace her.

"It was nice meeting you Susan. I wish it was a happier occasion, but maybe I will have some good news later." Freda turned to hug Thomas before leaving.

"I need to meet with a few other friends," Thomas said, reaching over to Susan and grasping her hand. "You've been through enough today. I'll take you somewhere to rest."

Susan wiped tears from her face. "Thanks for everything, Thomas."

****

Thomas took Susan to a quiet hotel, stopping to buy clean clothes and two new cell phones. "You'll be safe here," he said, as they stepped inside the hotel room. "The owner is a friend of Raheem." He sat on the side of the bed looking down at his cell phone. "I'm sending you my number." Susan's phone beeped. "Keep your head inside and you'll be fine."

Susan nodded.

"I'll be back around 6pm. Take this." He held out a small handgun he had taken from a security guard at the palace. "I hope you won't need to use it."

Susan examined the gun. "Stay safe, Thomas."

Thomas gave her a reassuring hug. "Don't worry, we'll find Kim."

****

An hour later, crouched behind some bushes, Thomas observed an address that Freda had given him. Sitting nearby, with his back to Thomas, Kameel, a faithful friend with short curly hair and a love for Hawaiian shirts, examined his finger nails. His bright colored shirt, gave him the appearance of a tourist on a pacific cruise. Several men entered the house and Thomas made a phone call. Within a few minutes, several police cars had arrived. Thomas threw a small stone at Kameel and pointed. The police cars eventually left and soon after, the men staying at the house also started to leave.

"One fake tip off, and they're leaving their hole," Thomas said.

He examined each face through his binoculars. Two men escorted a woman with brown wavy hair into one of two cars outside. He touched the communicator in his ear and spoke to the others he had recruited. "Pharaoh is on the move. The Princess is mobile."

"Are you sure that's Kim?" Kameel asked.

"That's her," Thomas confirmed.

They followed the men on Thomas' bike until the traffic was almost at a standstill. Passengers waved flags and drivers honked their horns in a slow-moving procession through the streets.

"Where did all these cars come from?" Kameel asked. "I asked the local soccer club if they could organise a street parade for us. Raheem is a big sponsor."

Kameel laughed.

"Okay guys, next intersection."

They moved slowly between the procession of vehicles till they were directly behind the two Egyptian's cars.

"On the count of three." Thomas moved his bike forward. "One." He squeezed the accelerator and moved to the side of one of the vehicles. "Two." Kameel jumped from the bike as Thomas moved level with the driver. "Now!"

Two other masked men surrounded the vehicles, smashing the driver's windows and taking the Egyptians by surprise. Thomas placed his gun against the driver's head and reached inside to remove the keys. He glanced back toward the second car. Kameel waved, indicating he had control of the car. Kim sat between two men in the back seat with masking tape over her mouth. Thomas opened the back door and waved his pistol, forcing one of the men to the ground.

"Stay there!"

As he reached for Kim's arm, a series of shots exploded from behind, causing him to take cover at the front of the vehicle. One of his team, lay on the ground motionless. Thomas looked down at blood oozing through his new shirt and ran backward to an abandoned taxi. The kidnappers left the cars and made their way along the street on foot, still holding Kim. Thomas slammed his fist against the side of the taxi, frustrated by his own incompetence.

"Kameel?"

"I'm okay here. Tariq took a hit but he's alive. Jamal …"

Thomas ran to remove the ammunition clip from the gun of his dead team member. "They're heading to Tit Mellil airport. It's only a few minutes away. We have to stop them."

"I'm with you man, but we'll need a shortcut," Kameel said. "Any ideas?"

Sirens squealed behind them as police arrived. Thomas and Kameel jumped on a bike, took a shortcut through a narrow alley, and manoeuvred their way through the traffic. They reached the airport in record time and hid their bike a short distance from the security fence.

"We're looking for a private plane that seats at least eight people," Thomas said, laying in a patch of long grass.

Kameel pointed to two DC30's.

"That's them. How much ammunition do you have?" Thomas asked.

"Just one round."

"I'm thinking we go in, create as much chaos as we can, and make sure this place is crawling with security before the other thugs arrive."

Kameel loaded the last of his ammunition. "Do we have an exit plan?"

Thomas started walking toward the security fence. "Not yet."

"God have mercy," Kameel said, looking up.

"Put that gun away," Thomas said. "I was joking about the guns."

Kameel's face wrinkled. "You almost had me," he said, shaking his head.

Thomas strained to lift a small part of the fence. "See if you can slide under."

Kameel reluctantly lay on his stomach and slid under. "Now your turn, Tommy," he said, pulling at the fence.

Thomas crawled under, ripping his shirt and leaving a deep cut in the process. "My body is taking a beating today" he said, groaning as he pulled his legs through. He lifted his shirt to examine the wound.

"Just a scratch," Kameel said smugly.

The scratch was just above an old scar. A reminder of his service in Iraq. An exploding grenade had dented his body in several places during a road ambush. Thomas wiped the blood.

They reached a nearby building, and after looking around, they made their way toward the DC30's parked nearby.

"We need a distraction while one of us gets to those planes," Thomas said.

Kameel smiled. "I have an idea."

"No guns blazing."

Kameel winked. "No guns blazing," he said, but before they could move, two vehicles entered the main gate.

"We have company," Thomas said.

"Guns blazing now, Tommy?"

"We have to stop that plane from taking off," Thomas replied, ignoring the joke. "And make sure that Kim isn't hurt," He pointed to some steel drums. "Cover me on the left!" He ran to the drums, in a position opposite Kameel.

Moments later, the two cars were racing toward them. Signalling Kameel, and running toward one of the planes, Thomas fired several shots at the cockpit. The window exploded, scattering shards of glass on the ground. As the cars sped closer, one of the occupants leaned from a window and fired bullets in their direction. Thomas dived behind a parked airport vehicle to avoid being hit.

"Hold on Tommy!" Kameel said, shooting several shots into the front of the first car. The cars stopped a short distance away and returned fire. One of the Egyptians stepped from the second car using Kim as a shield, and the group made their way to the second plane. Kameel hit one of the men in the shoulder, but concerned for Kim's safety, he stopped. As the plane taxied down the runway, the two men watched on helplessly.

CHAPTER 12

Tamarindo, Costa Rica

CRUSE, YOU BASTARD!" Susan yelled, throwing a glass sugar bowl across the room. The bowl broke into several pieces and scattered sugar over the floor. Two exhausting weeks travelling the smuggler's route to avoid border security, had left her tired and frustrated. She had waited two days for Thomas, but after receiving no contact, she had returned to Costa Rica. Visiting Paris had seemed so exciting only a few weeks ago, today she had returned licking her wounds like a defeated dog. She looked at her handbag on the dining table. There was nothing to unpack. She made her way to the bedroom, collapsing in tears on her bed, and holding her pillow for comfort. Several hours later, she woke to the sound of knocking.

"Susan, it's me, Maria!"

She wiped her eyes and moved sluggishly toward the door. As she opened the door, sunlight bathed her face.

Maria held a bunch of flowers and a jar of homemade jam.

"I'm sorry if I woke you. I heard that you had returned and wanted to bring a small gift."

"Thanks so much, Maria." She reached around the bunch of flowers to hug her. "Come in."

Maria placed her gifts on the kitchen table.

"How is your family?" Susan asked.

"They'll all well. Antonio played his first soccer game this week."

"That sounds exciting," Susan said, wiping the sleep from her eyes. "You must be proud of him."

"And how was your trip?"

Susan looked downward. "It didn't end very well." Tears came to her eyes.

Maria hugged her. "Come and join us for dinner tonight."

"That sounds nice," Susan replied, wiping her eyes.

Maria hugged Susan silently for several minutes before excusing herself. "I wish I could stay longer."

"Thanks again for the flowers and jam."

"See you tonight."

****

The aroma of food greeted Susan as she approached Maria's house. Antonio, aged eight, answered the door with his younger sister shyly clinging to his side. Susan held out a small chocolate cake she had brought, and Antonio received it with a large grin.

"Mama, look what Susan brought," he said, carefully carrying the cake to the kitchen, where Maria was chopping chives for the meal. A set of golden saucepans decorated each of the kitchen walls.

"Susan! It's so wonderful to have you with us," Maria said, dropping her knife to embrace her. "Take a seat in the lounge. I'll be with you in a minute."

"Can I do anything to help?"

"No, no, I'm almost finished," Maria replied. "You go relax. I'll join you in a minute."

As Susan sat questioning the children about their week, Maria's husband Anton, arrived.

"Susan, how are you?" he said, removing his jacket.

Susan stood to greet him with a kiss on the cheek.

"I'm well. How is your work?" she asked.

"Work is going well." Anton positioned himself on the corner of a lounge chair opposite Susan. His large body frame balanced awkwardly on the leather upholstery. "We're looking for another admin person if you're interested."

Susan laughed. "I'm afraid my typing is still quite slow in Spanish."

"Honey, please get Susan a drink!" Maria called, from the kitchen.

"What would you like to drink?" he asked, giving her several options. "I can also make your favourite fruit punch."

"Fruit punch!" the children shouted in unison.

"The punch sounds great," Susan said, reaching out for Hanna to sit on her lap.

Maria finally entered the lounge and announced the meal was ready. The dining room was much smaller than Raheem's palace, but Susan loved the family environment. After everyone was seated, Maria looked at her husband. Anton waited for the children to bow their heads.

"Dear Lord, we thank you for this wonderful meal tonight, for everything you provide for us, and for Susan, our beautiful guest." Suddenly, Antonio sneezed, breaking the silence. "Amen!"

Hanna laughed loudly. "Antonio sounds like a dog sneezing." She giggled in her high-pitched voice, and the room erupted with laughter.

"Tell us about your trip, Susan," Maria asked.

Susan's head dropped.

"You visited your family?" Anton asked.

Susan moved uncomfortably in her chair. "It didn't quite work out the way I had planned."

Maria looked at Anton and back at Susan. "Roses are covered in thorns. When you reach out to pick one, sometimes you end up with just a thorn."

"Ouch," Hanna said, pulling a painful face. "Did you get a sore finger?"

Maria raised her finger to silence Hanna.

Susan wiped her eyes. "I've felt so many thorns the last few years."

Maria moved her chair closer and reached her arm around Susan to offer comfort.

"Sometimes it all seems too overwhelming."

"Inside the cocoon, every caterpillar feels uncertainty," Maria said, touching the side of Susan's cheek, "But after enough time passes, the cocoon breaks open, and the world sees its true beauty." Maria paused to stare into Susan's eyes. "When the caterpillar feels the darkness, all is well." She looked at Anton for support.

"The world will see your beauty. Wait and see," he said.

Hanna pulled her father's arm. "Father, is Susan going to turn into a butterfly?"

The room erupted in laughter.

"No darling, Susan looks fine the way she is."

Maria moved closer to hug Susan, and the mood of the room changed to laughter and smiles.

Later that night, Susan lay in bed reflecting on the encouraging words that Maria had shared. She opened a small bible that Anton had previously given her. Susan had always admired Anton and Maria's faith. Aside from Kim and Alfred, they were perhaps the most spiritual people she had ever met. She turned the pages of the small book and read a line that Maria had underlined for her, "For such a time as this."

****

The next morning, the sun shone on Susan's bed, causing her to squint. It was a rare event when she overslept. She rolled over, fumbling for the small bible and returning to the underlined verse. The words, 'For such a time', replayed through her head. She returned the bible to the small wooden table at her bedside and walked to the lounge room. Leaning down, she removed a leather cushion from her couch and lifted away the thin cloth covering the chair frame. Inside, there were several small white bags. Susan removed one of the bags and stood. "For such a time as this," she said, removing a thick roll of American $100 notes.

CHAPTER 13

SUSAN LOOKED THROUGH the open window of her taxi. It was a typical business day. Nobody was in a rush. No traffic jams. It was this slow-paced lifestyle that had worked its magic when she first arrived in Tamarindo. The taxi finally stopped outside a small computer store and she handed the driver a $10 note. At the shop entrance, a young man stood stroking his short rough beard.

"Susan, how are you?" He welcomed her inside, and past a row of new computers. The back wall was full of empty boxes, freshly opened. "Excuse the mess, I just received new stock. Are you interested in a look?" He smiled optimistically, pointing to a new computer.

Susan laughed. "I'm sorry. No upgrades today. I just need to search for something on the internet, but I need to do it anonymously."

"No problems." He led her to his work area. "What you need is a proxy chain to mask your IP address."

"So, you can do some geeky stuff and hide my identity?"

"That's correct." He sat at his desk which resembled the cockpit of a small plane. "Grab a chair." Three large monitors formed a semicircle in front of him. To the right side of the desk, several lights pulsed green and orange colours. Susan's eyes scanned the desk, which was full of magazines, and food wrappers. Jose pushed a pile of magazines to the side.

"So, no one will know we have searched?" Susan confirmed.

"Well, the site owner will know that someone has made a search, but they will have to work hard to trace our location, if that makes sense." He opened several browsing windows.

"That's great," Susan said, looking around the shop as Jose continued to tap his keyboard.

Jose lowered his voice. "Don't tell anyone, but I use this method for downloading movies."

"Cross my heart."

Jose glanced up with a puzzled look. "Hail Mary. Cross on your heart?" He continued to tap his keyboard.

Susan laughed. "It means I promise not to tell."

"Okaaaay." Jose's voice was monotone, as if making a mental note. He finally looked up again, raising his eyebrows with curiosity. "So, what are we searching for?"

"I have a list of names. I need to know who they are," she said. "Please don't ask why."

He smiled. "No problems. Cross on my bum."

Susan held out the list of names and ignored his bum comment.

"Okay, what have we got here?" he said, glancing at the names. "Duncan Volker." He typed the name and scrolled through a list of sites. "What are we looking for?" he asked.

"Well, if possible, an address, and any background information about him."

"Do we know any other details that might help narrow the search results?"

"He's possibly working in the technology industry."

Jose stroked his beard. "Hmm, let's try that." He clicked on a page. "This guy's address is easy to find." Jose looked at Susan. "I hope he wasn't family."

Susan read aloud, "Munich cemetery, Germany. He died two years ago."

"Let's see how he died," Jose said, opening several more links. "Here's something."

"A car crash," Susan said, reading the headline.

Jose scrolled down the page. "He was a scientist. Made some important improvements for modern radar systems. Interesting guy."

Susan pointed at the list again. "What about this one?"

Jose typed the name, "Roderick Durtire," and clicked on a link. "Another scientist. This guy had some pretty serious awards," he said, staring at his monitor.

"What do you mean, 'had'?"

"He lived in Paris, won a heap of awards for his research in laser technology, and died two and a half years ago in a house fire."

Jose looked around. "Who else is on that list?"

"Try Matthew Goldman."

"Okay, Matthew Goldman. Let's see." He clicked on several links.

"Manager at a shoe factory, another guy who sells fish tanks."

"What about Golman?"

"So, same name without the d?" Jose confirmed.

"Yes, without the d."

He retyped the name and opened several links before turning to look at Susan.

"These are some seriously cool people. Where did you get their names?"

Susan returned a blank stare.

"I know, I know. Cross my bum." He laughed and returned to face his monitor. "I hope these aren't guys you met from an online dating site, cause at this rate you'll be single the rest of your life." He continued laughing.

"Why do you say that?"

"Matthew Golman died six months ago." He pointed at the monitor on his left.

"I have a list of dead men?" Susan asked.

"It looks that way. Golman drowned in a backyard swimming pool. Apparently, he was drunk at the time."

"What type of work did he do?"

"It says here that he was an electronic engineer. Worked with all the big companies." He tapped the computer casing. "He probably helped design some of the circuit boards in this computer."

"What about the last guy," Susan said. "Max Townsend."

"Okay, there's probably 5000 Max Townsend's, but I'm searching for dead scientists, right?" He looked at Susan with a silly grin.

Susan thumped him in the arm, but secretly enjoyed his sense of humour. "Let's start with those still living."

"Hmmm, this is interesting," he said, pointing to the monitor on his left.

"What do you have?"

"Max went missing two years ago. He was scheduled to give a lecture at a London university and didn't show up. No one's seen him since." He clicked various links. "He's published several articles on plasma technology and won some prestigious innovation awards."

"His father is a watchmaker in Venice?" Susan said, pointing at another link.

He tapped the keyboard and opened another window. "It looks like he just celebrated his birthday a few days ago."

"Max had a birthday?"

"No, his father had a birthday." Jose leaned backward in his chair. "The old man just turned 90."

Susan raised her eyebrows as she scanned the article.

"If we can find him, there might still be hope for your love life," Jose said, winking at Susan.

"So, where can I find Max?"

Before Jose could reply, a customer entered the shop, interrupting the conversation. "Just a minute," he said, excusing himself and leaving Susan to stare at the monitor.

She studied Max's photo. The short brown hair, beard and glasses reminded her of her father. His eyebrows met in the middle. "Can we find an address for Max's father?" Susan asked, as Jose returned.

"Okay. Watchmakers in Venice." He entered the search words.

"Here we go. Fred Townsend's Antique Clocks. That's our guy." He looked up with a pleased smile.

"That's awesome!" Susan wrote down the address. "Now what?"

"Visit the father and ask him to organise a date with his son."

Susan gave him a playful slap on the back.

Jose laughed. "I can't help you with that. I don't run a matchmaking service." He stood to his feet laughing.

"Thanks for the help. What do I owe you?" she asked.

"No charge today. Just make sure you remember me when you want a new computer."

"Are you sure?"

"Yes, I'm sure. Just promise me you'll stop by and visit again soon."

"I will," she said, turning to leave.

"Cross on your bum."

Susan twisted her lip in a comical frown. Jose followed her to the door, still laughing.

On the way back to her apartment, Susan wondered how many of the names on the Flashlight list had met the same fate as the men she had just searched for. There was one more stop on the way home. The local travel agent.

CHAPTER 14

Venice, Italy

ALTHOUGH IT WAS lightly raining, the damp air and mist only added to the beauty of Venice. An eloquently dressed porter took Susan's bag and welcomed her at the hotel entrance. Inside, a short brunette greeted her at the reception.

"I have a booking for Mr. and Mrs. Lenard Dior."

"Can I see your passport?" Susan searched her handbag. "I'm sorry, my husband must have it. He was in a rush to attend a business meeting and usually keeps both passports in his briefcase."

The receptionist smiled. "It's okay Madam, your husband can drop the passports in when he comes."

"Thank you so much. I will message him from my room."

Susan signed the entry book, while the porter took the keycard and bag, and led her to the room. He sat the bag on a table near her bed and smiled politely. "Enjoy your stay. If you need further assistance please call us."

"Thanks. I'm sure I'll enjoy my visit." Susan handed him a generous tip, and he left the room. She opened the doors to the balcony, and the cold winter air hit her face. The main canal was in clear view. It had been Kim's desire to visit Venice after Paris. Paris seemed such a distant memory now. Reaching into her pocket she removed a small note with Fred Townsend's address. It wasn't much, but at least she had a small lead.

A short time later, Susan stepped onto the red carpet leading to the street and unfolded a map. After thirty minutes walking through the cobblestone streets, she arrived at a small shop. The front window was filled with a variety of old clocks and watches. A small bell chimed as she entered. The shop was in a poor state, and probably hadn't been cleaned for several years. Mr. Townsend was obviously continuing his business as a personal hobby these days. Susan looked around the shop and stared at the old man sitting behind a small counter. He had a cheerful smile, a wisp of grey hair neatly combed to one side, and a red patterned shirt.

"Congratulations on your birthday."

He looked up and she pointed to a row of birthday cards still sitting on a shelf.

He gave a croaky laugh. "Thank you. I'm not getting any younger."

"How long have you had the shop?" she asked, looking around the room.

"Almost 20 years."

"You're English?"

"Yes. English with a bad Italian accent." He laughed again. "My wife and I loved to visit Venice for holidays. After she died, I moved here."

"You have some interesting old clocks."

He stood from his wooden stool and moved toward a beautiful clock on Susan's left. "This is my favourite. It's a gift from a friend. Built in 1760, and once owned by Catherine the Great."

Susan admired the detailed workmanship. "It's beautiful."

"There's a rumour that Catherine received it from one of her secret lovers."

He shuffled back toward his stool. "Do you know how many secret lovers Catherine the Great had?"

Susan shook her head.

"Some say she had over 300 men!"

Susan's eyes widened. "How on earth did she remember all their names?"

The old man laughed again. "I think that's a question only a woman can answer." He laughed. "Well, is there anything I can help you with, young lady?"

"I was hoping you might know where I could find a friend."

"And who might that be?"

Susan stared into Mr. Townsend's eyes. "Your son."

The old man looked down toward his work bench. "I'm sorry miss. I can't help you." His tone expressed a reluctance to talk further.

"I don't want to cause any trouble."

The old man picked up a small tool from his desk. "Maybe it's best that you go," he said, while cleaning an old watch.

Susan turned to leave, stopping to look at the old man as she reached the door. Further down the street, Susan sat by the window in a small coffee shop, trying to piece together what she already knew. She wrote 'Venice' on a napkin and stared out the window as a gondola sailed past in the canal. Mr. Townsend's reluctance to talk about his son, seemed to confirm that she was on the right track.

"Can I get anything else for you?"

Susan shook her head. As the waitress left, a tear formed in her eye as she remembered Raheem and Thomas. She held her emotions, turning her thoughts once again to Max Townsend. If Max was still alive and in hiding, he would probably choose a different career than his past. Susan was sure he had learned to fix old clocks from his father. Perhaps he had even sent his father the clock from Russia. She sipped her coffee and wrote on the napkin again.

On her return to Fred Townsend's shop, she read the napkin in her hand. 'Venice, no close family, Max, risk, clocks, Catherine the Great, Russia?' The little bell sounded its familiar chime as Susan entered the small shop once again. "I'm sorry, Mr. Townsend. I've lost one of my gloves." She scanned the shop.

"Gloves," the old man mumbled. "Lost gloves." He returned to cleaning the watch on his bench and Susan seized the opportunity to grab several birthday cards from a nearby shelf. Memorizing the male names, she quickly returned the cards. After circling the shop, she checked several more cards and waved a small leather glove in the air.

"Found it."

The old man grunted his acknowledgement.

"Goodbye, Mr. Townsend."

The old man continued with his work without looking. "Lost gloves," he mumbled.

The door closed, and Susan peered through the shop window one last time. Around the corner, she stopped to write seven names on the reverse side of her napkin. One of these men might know Max and be helping him. It was a long shot, but worth investigating.

Inside her hotel room, she searched for each of the names online. One of the men was an old friend from England. There were several locals, one who owned a neighbouring store, and a German sounding name, Fredrick Bremer. Susan examined the search list for Fredrick Bremer, and then narrowed the search by adding 'Watchmaker'. She relaxed in her chair and stared at one of the addresses.

"Saint Petersburg, Russia."

CHAPTER 15

Saint Petersburg, Russia

A WOMAN WEARING a yellow and green headscarf tapped Susan's leg and pointed at the door. "Ploshad Lenina."

As the underground train came to a stop, Susan thanked the woman and stepped onto the platform. A continuous line of people moved up and down the escalators leading to the exit. Susan watched the endless line of people travelling down the escalator in the opposite direction. Some of the faces reminded her of friends she had known in New York. Outside it was still snowing. She walked through the blanket of fresh snow covering the sidewalk, creating a small trail behind her.

A young couple offered her directions, and ten minutes later, she stood outside a small store. According to her research, watchmakers had been making a comeback in Russia. Susan entered the store and approached the counter. "Hello. Do you speak English?"

"One moment."

The young cashier disappeared through a door behind her and a short moment later, a bald-headed man with glasses and a moustache entered.

"Hello, can I help you?" he asked, speaking fluent English.

"Mr. Bremer?"

"Yes, that's me." He pressed his lips together defensively.

Susan reached out her hand. "Diana Smith." She looked at his assistant. "I need to speak to you alone."

He signalled Susan to follow him into the back room. "Come through." The room was filled with shelves containing boxes of watch parts. He positioned a seat for her. "How can I help you?"

"I'm looking for a friend who might be living here in Russia."

"Okay; and you think I might know him?"

"Yes." Susan moved slightly forward on her seat. "I believe my friend is working with watches here St. Petersburg. He's an English speaker, and probably moved here in the last two years."

Fredrick tilted his head to one side and looked at Susan suspiciously. "Does he have a name?"

"Max. Max Townsend."

Fredrick shook his head. "I don't know anyone by that name."

"If you know something Mr. Bremer…."

Fredrick interrupted. "Look, I don't know who you are, what you want, or whether I even want to trust you."

"I'm only after some answers that might help a friend," Susan pleaded.

Fredrick stood to escort her outside. "I'm sorry, but I can't help you."

"I've just come from Venice and visited Max's father."

Fredrick bowed his head and rolled his eyes upward at Susan, as if in a trance. "Why should I trust you?" he finally said.

Susan thought for a moment. "My real name is Susan Banks. My husband was murdered in New York. I need answers."

Fredrick remained silent.

"I believe Max Townsend can help me," she said.

He stared at Susan. "I recognise your face. I'm sorry about your husband." He paused. "I hope I'm right in trusting you."

"Mr. Bremer, I give you my word. No one knows I'm even in the country."

Fredrick placed his hands in his pockets and stared at her. "Meet me here again tomorrow at 11am. I'll see what I can find out. Keep out of sight, and don't let anyone know you've visited me."

Susan nodded. "11am tomorrow."

"That's right."

Susan turned at the door. "Thank you. Spasibo."

Fredrick lifted his hand. "Proshchay."

******

The next morning, as Susan sat eating breakfast, she was interrupted by a voice behind her.

"Excuse me."

She turned, expecting to see a waiter.

"Miss Smith?"

She looked up. "Yes."

"My name is Mathias Schmidt. Fredrick sent me."

"Please." She motioned him to sit, observing him as he removed his coat. Within a few seconds, she recognised the nose, and distinctive eye brows. He had lost his beard. "Max?"

Max removed the scarf from his neck and took a seat.

"How did you know I was here?" she said.

He scanned the room, ignoring her question. "I knew Alfred, and I read about his death."

Susan savoured the moment, hardly believing she was sitting across the table from someone who knew Alfred. "You know about Flashlight?"

"Yes, that's the reason I changed my identity and left England," he said. "How did you find me?"

"Just a lucky guess." Susan stared at his broad chin. "I thought you might own a shop or be working with someone who sold old clocks; like your father."

"You visited my father?"

"Yes, he's a lovely man. He was very tight-lipped." She smiled. "But I knew he might be trying to protect you."

"How is he?"

"He looks well. He loved the clock you sent."

Max looked at Susan with a puzzled expression. "I never sent any clock."

"Your father had his ninetieth birthday a few months ago."

"Susan, I haven't been in contact with my father for over two years."

Susan leaned forward. "Really?" She sat back in her chair contemplating the outcome of her wild guess. "I know what it's like," she finally replied, "I haven't seen my family or friends for over two years either."

"It's hard not being able to communicate with people you care about," Max said.

"So, what can you tell me about Flashlight?"

Max rolled his shoulders and rubbed the back of his neck. "Not much really. Someone tried to kidnap me, so I went into hiding." He paused. "I read the news online. All of my research team were killed or went missing." He stared into her eyes. "All of them. 13 colleagues."

Susan leaned forward. "You reported it to the police?"

"I informed the police. They took a description of the attacker but said they couldn't offer protection."

"Can you remember the date?" Susan asked.

"It was about a month before Alfred's death."

"So, Cruse started killing or kidnapping the world's top scientists about two years ago."

"Who's Cruse?"

"A CIA boss," Susan said. "We believe he's behind the disappearances."

Max moved in his chair. "I know where Cruse would be," he said.

Susan's eyes widened. "Really?"

Max's eyes glazed over in a trance.

"Max?"

He leaned forward to whisper. "Delta Bunker."

"What's Delta Bunker?"

"All the people on the Flashlight list have expertise in technology research."

"Go ahead."

"If any of them are still alive, they would be at Delta." He paused. "It's an underground research bunker in the Nevada desert."

"How do you know about this… Delta Bunker?"

"I knew someone who worked there for a few years. He's dead now."

"Sorry."

"No, no, it's not like that. Harold died of old age. He was 87."

"Your uncle?"

"Good guess." Max relaxed in his chair. "Uncle Harold was the one that inspired me to study science and technology."

"So, how do I find Delta Bunker?"

Max laughed. "You won't get anywhere near a CIA bunker." He changed the tone of his voice. "Not if you want to stay alive."

Susan's mind was racing. "Kim and Alfred could be alive somewhere under the Nevada desert?"

"Susan, forget it. The CIA has everyone around their finger. The safest thing is to stay out of their way and forget this conversation." He looked her directly in the eyes. "I've lost a lot of friends." He shook his head. "I don't want to be the next." He rose abruptly from the table and grabbed his coat. "Please forget this meeting. I have..." He stared at Susan. "I don't want trouble."

"I won't bother you again," she promised.

He wrapped the scarf around his neck and looked at her one last time.

"Bye, Susan. Stay safe."

CHAPTER 16

Delta Bunker, Nevada Desert

SCOTT DENMAN ENTERED the surveillance room with his assistant Michelle, following close behind.

"Okay, what've we got people?" he said, commanding attention.

"We received a match on Susan Banks about 30 minutes ago," Drew answered.

"Banks?" He looked around the room. "Where?"

"Moscow's underground metro." Drew pointed to the large wall monitor. "This picture was taken from a security camera inside Chekhovskaya Metro."

Scott stared at Susan's picture.

"It's been confirmed. This is definitely Susan Banks."

Scott paced the room. "Why Moscow? I want everyone on this! Connect me to Moscow."

A few minutes later, one of the staff approached Scott with a handset. "Sir, Donaldson from Moscow."

Scott placed the call on loudspeaker. "Steve, this is Scott Denman. What's happening?"

"We received a match on a priority target, Susan Banks. Four of our teams are currently searching for her."

"Steve, we appreciate your eyes on the ground."

"So, what are we dealing with?" Donaldson asked.

"She's not considered dangerous, but so far she's managed to evade capture."

"We'll hardwire you into our communications," Donaldson said, eager to earn favour with Scott. In this business, the more friends you had, the better.

Moscow, Russia

Unaware that she was being followed, Susan stepped inside a small grocery shop looking for tissues. Several customers stood at the cashier as she browsed the aisles. As she stood in the cosmetic section, a man in a large black overcoat entered the store. She felt his stare and turned away. A minute later, as Susan approached the checkout, the man was flicking through magazines. Susan's palms were sweating as she waited in line.

The cashier took Susan's tissues and placed them in a small bag. "Pyat' dollarov," she said, holding up five fingers.

Susan held out a two hundred ruble note and glanced nervously toward the magazine rack. As the cashier searched for change, a local bus stopped outside. Seeing an opportunity, Susan ran from the shop. The cashier held out her hand with several coins and yelled, alerting the man in the overcoat. As he reached the door, the bus moved forward. Following his instincts, he sprinted along the road chasing the bus. He was joined by another man from across the street, who also ran to intercept the bus. Both men were screaming in Russian, with the largest man banging on the side of the bus. Unnoticed, Susan peered through the window of a neighbouring store.

"Help me," she said, addressing the store owner, a woman in her fifties with brown hair and smokers' wrinkles. The woman looked toward the street where the men were shouting at the bus, then taking Susan's hand, she led her into a back room.

"Ostavaysya zdes," she said, waving her hand for Susan to sit, and returning to her front counter.

Susan looked around the tiny room. A thick brown coat hung on a hook near the back door. She quickly changed coats and grabbed a black scarf on a nearby bench. The rear door creaked open and Susan peered outside to check her surroundings. Outside, she followed a path along the main river, and made her way toward a large crowd of people who were gathered outside a cathedral.

Delta Bunker, Nevada Desert

"Donaldson's team are confirming they have lost visual contact."

Scott slammed his fist on a desk. "Damn!" He shook his head in frustration. "Donaldson better not screw this."

One of Scott's team pointed to a live camera feed. "There she is. St. Basil's Cathedral." As they watched, Susan disappeared among the crowd.

"Send the link to Moscow!" Scott shouted, pacing the room, while Drew turned up the volume on the live link.

"Unit 3 at St. Basil's. We're going in. Requesting backup."

Scott shook his head. "She won't be in the church. There aren't enough exits."

They watched the monitors as two agents pushed through the crowd and ran toward the church.

Moscow, Russia

Joining a small group of women, Susan moved away from the church and spotted a dry-cleaning van. The back door of the van was opened and two men were loading bundles of clothing into the truck. Susan walked past the back of the van and quickly jumped into the front. As she waited in the passenger seat, it started snowing.

Suddenly, the driver's door swung open. The startled driver yelled something in Russian. Susan held a 2000 ruble note toward the man.

"I am cold. Please give me a lift," she said.

The man jumped behind the wheel, taking the money as he started the engine. He mumbled something in Russian. Susan sat quietly, not knowing what to say, and not caring about the destination. As a police car passed from the opposite direction, she slid down into her seat.

Delta Bunker, Nevada Desert

Scott ran a hand through his hair in frustration. "Come on, damn it!" The New York clubhouse incident was still a sting of embarrassment in his mind. He hated looking like a fool.

"Give me a private line." He said, leaving the room with the handset. "Steve, Scott here. What's happening?"

"Our teams have a perimeter around St. Basil's," Donaldson said.

Scott closed the door of his room. "Steve, is this a private line?"

"I'm just moving into the hallway."

"What I'm about to tell you is off the record."

Donaldson's tone deepened to reflect Scott's seriousness. "Okay, I'm listening."

"Susan Banks has already managed to make my team look like complete idiots." He paused. "She has somehow managed to evade us for almost two years, even though she has no special training."

"Why is she so important?"

"We have reason to believe that she has sensitive information relating to a program being run out of our technology division. We call it, 'Flashlight'. The information she has could disrupt our whole operation."

"You want teams on all borders, and…"

Scott interrupted. "I want everything you can give me, Steve. If you can put a team at every metro station in Moscow, do it."

"200 stations?" Donaldson asked.

"Just help me close this, and you can name your price." Scott said, trying to pump up Donaldson's commitment level.

"Okay, I get you. We'll do all we can."

"Just keep your eyes open, she could be working with one of our former agents," Scott said. "I'll send you the full background report of Thomas Lansdowne. He's ex-CIA, last seen with Banks in Morocco a few months ago, and might still be working with her."

"Okay. Thanks," Donaldson said, refraining from further questions.

Scott stopped to reinforce his last point. "If we fail at this, Cruse will have both our heads on a meat platter."

Susan looked through the fogged windscreen at the snow falling. Her heart was still racing. After several intersections, she turned to look at the driver. His big fur hat looked out of place on his rugged body. The driver ignored her. After travelling through the streets for ten minutes, the van stopped and the man held up his hand.

"Ostavaysya zdes."

"I get it. Stay here," Susan replied.

The man muttered the phrase a second time, and then left the van. Susan heard voices, and the sound of the back door opening. Several minutes later, the driver was back and they were moving again.

"Where go you?" the driver asked, in broken English.

Susan reached into her handbag and held up several American notes.

"Ukraine. I want to go to Ukraine."

He grabbed the money. "Ukraine?"

Susan nodded.

He glanced sideways again to confirm. "Ukraine?"

"Ukraine. I need to go to Ukraine," Susan repeated, hoping the man understood her.

They stopped at traffic lights a few minutes later, and he flicked the money through his fingers. Six fifty-dollar notes. He looked at Susan, nodded his head, and placed one of the notes in his pocket. As they moved through the traffic again, he dialled a number on his mobile. For the next few minutes he was deep in conversion. Susan stared out the window, turning her head and nodding each time she heard the word Ukraine. The man continued to talk, occasionally glancing at Susan to offer a reassuring nod.

A short time later, the van stopped outside a small furniture shop. "Ukraine," the man said, waving at Susan to exit the vehicle with him. He walked inside the store, waiting for Susan to follow him. Inside, a blast of warm air massaged Susan's face. The driver spoke to a young man, handing him the money and pointing in Susan's direction. The young man counted the money, nodding his head as he listened to the older man's instructions. After talking for several minutes, the young man shook the driver's hand and led Susan through the shop and out a back exit. They approached a small grey Lada, a remnant of the communist era, with rust around the bottom.

"I speak English, little bit," he said, opening the passenger door for Susan.

CHAPTER 17

Moscow, Russia

SUSAN GLANCED ACROSS at her new driver. He had an attractive three-day beard and welcoming eyes. His thick blue ski jacket and black scarf, in contrast to the car they were in, was very modern.

"What is your name?" she asked.

He pulled his beanie down over the tips of his ears. "Vladimir."

"Vlad-i-mir."

He nodded.

"I'm Diane."

Susan adjusted her collar to help guard her neck against the cold breeze rushing through the loose windows.

"Was that your uncle in the store?"

"My uncle?"

"Never mind. The main thing is that we are heading toward Ukraine."

"Yes, I take you, Ukraine." He reached forward to turn up the music volume. "American music." He smiled as the song played and pointed at Susan. "American?"

"Yes, I'm American," she said, raising her voice over the music. "How long is it to Ukraine?"

Vladimir's forehead creased in a puzzled expression.

"How many hours will we travel?"

He took a cloth and leaned forward to wipe condensation from the windscreen. "We travel Ukraine, five hours."

Susan leaned back into her seat. With Vladimir's choice of hip-hop music; it would be a long unforgettable trip, but hopefully without anyone following.

Langley, Virginia

Cruse reached for his stress ball, squeezing it tight. He was in his typical bad mood. "What's happening, Scott?" he said, with a demanding tone.

Scott held the phone receiver and rocked his chair from side to side. "We have a development with Flashlight."

"I'm listening."

Scott lifted a sheet of paper from his desk. "Early this morning, Banks showed up in Moscow." His free hand formed a tense fist.

"Airport security?"

"There's no record of her entering the country." Scott rolled closer toward his desk. "She must have jumped a border somewhere, most likely Ukraine."

"Okay, stay on this. Do whatever it takes to bring her in alive. If she has the flash drive, or knows where it is, we need to get it. And we need to know if there's other copies."

Scott pushed his chair backward. "I have a team leaving for Ukraine in two and a half hours."

"Great! Don't let me down again, Scott."

Kiyevskoye Highway, Russia

A few hours later, Vladimir eased his small car off the highway toward a petrol station. "Almost half way," he said.

Susan stepped from the car, stretched her legs, and walked toward a small café. A large black limousine was parked a short distance away. Inside, a well-dressed man and woman were sitting at a table drinking coffee. A beautiful dark brown coat hung over the back of the woman's chair. Three years ago, Susan had been working in a legal office, helping to bring justice to society. Now, she was planning to steal another coat. Two in one day.

As Susan left the bathroom, the woman who owned the coat was standing at the checkout. Susan approached the woman's husband and pointed at the Limo outside. "Is that your car?"

"No understand," he said.

"Oil running everywhere," Susan said, using her arms to dramatize her story.

He rose to his feet, looking outside with curiosity.

"Your car. Tvoya mashina," she said, hoping he would investigate. He finally took the bait and disappeared outside. Susan turned to the cashier who was serving the woman, and seizing a moment when no one was looking, she grabbed the unattended coat. She tossed her previous coat on a nearby table and hurried out the door.

Vladimir had refuelled and was leaning against the back of his car enjoying a cigarette with another man. Without looking at him, Susan entered the car and hit the horn to indicate she was ready to leave. Both men looked around, startled by the sound. Susan hit the horn again.

"Okay, Okay, one minute," Vladimir said, smiling at the other man.

Susan checked the rear-view mirror. On the opposite side of the car park, the unsuspecting man was walking around the outside of his Limo. Susan felt the soft fur of the coat and immediately recognized its value.

Delta Bunker, Nevada Desert

Meanwhile, in a meeting room deep underground, Scott placed his briefcase beside his chair. "Okay people, listen up." The room went quiet. "Susan Banks." He opened a file in front of him. "Drew, give us a brief rundown of what we know so far."

Drew stood and approached the front of the room. "For those who are new, Banks is an agency priority." He displayed several pictures of Susan on a large monitor. "Her last known location was St. Basil Cathedral in Moscow. We believe her current location is somewhere South of Moscow, moving toward the Ukrainian border. There is no record of her entering the country, although we are still reviewing airport footage for the previous month." He looked around the room before continuing. "Her previous known locations have included Paris, Morocco, and New York, where she disappeared approximately two years ago. We believe she has information…"

Scott interrupted. "We believe she has information regarding Flashlight." He looked around the room. "I don't need to tell you how important this is."

Everyone nodded.

"Tell them about Lansdowne."

"Thomas Lansdowne, ex-CIA, trained by the best." Several pictures flashed on the monitor behind him. "He served several tours in Iraq and was awarded the Distinguished Service Cross for a mission in Afghanistan. Previous to being recruited by the CIA, he served with Delta force and led a covert operations team. He was recruited by us in 2010 and worked with the special operation group.

"Impressive record."

"He's well trained," Drew replied, looking up from his notes.

"Is he working with anyone else?"

"His last known whereabouts was Morocco, working as security advisor for a Saudi businessman, Raheem Ahmad. Ahmad was killed several months ago in a bungled operation to capture Banks. Susan Banks was a guest of Ahmad, and last seen with Lansdowne before her visit to Russia. Lansdowne's location is still unknown." He paused. "Any questions?"

"Do we know why Banks was in Moscow, and how long she was there?"

"We have video footage of Banks studying the metro plan in Moscow, which means this was probably her first visit. We still have no idea why she was in Moscow, but now that she's been spooked, we believe she will return to somewhere she is more comfortable. Perhaps Italy."

Drew looked around the room. "Any further questions?"

"Okay, listen up," Scott said. "I'm taking a team to Kiev in one hour. Marcus, Drew, Michelle and Jared, pack your bags, I want you guys on team. Greg, I want you to take charge of operations here, and give us support."

Greg was a recruit from the air force, and part of the operations team since its founding. His blond hair and pale skin made him stand out above the other members of the team.

"Toni, I also want you along to help with communication and translation. Any questions?" He scanned the room and checked the time. "Those on team, meet back here in thirty minutes. We leave for Kiev at 0200."

Russia

"A new coat," Vladimir said.

"You like it?"

"Ochen krasivaja."

Judging by the look in his eyes, Susan guessed he was impressed. She reached into the coat pockets, removing a small packet of tissues, a gold pen, and a small notepad. She held the pen closer and read the name engraved on the side. "Levinia." Vladimir glanced sideways without comment. Susan's fingers flipped through the pages of the small notepad, not able to understand anything, but admiring the handwriting. Somehow it felt worse now that the coat had a name attached to it. She knew how it felt losing something of value. Her mind drifted to memories of Tom. Life had seemed so perfect back in New York. She suddenly felt alone. At least Levinia still had her husband.

CHAPTER 18

Russian / Ukrainian border

SUSAN TIGHTENED THE scarf around her neck, and waved Vladimir farewell. She had been through the Ukrainian border once before, but this time she knew she was being followed. As Vladimir's small car drove away, Susan felt around the bottom of her handbag and removed the handgun that Thomas had given her in Morocco. She had practised daily until she could reload the gun in darkness. Holding the gun didn't remove the anxiety she was now feeling, but it helped. Minus ten degrees wasn't making it any easier. The cold winter air stung her nose as she walked through the streets contemplating her next move.

Atlas Hotel, Kiev, Ukraine

The door opened, and Marcus entered carrying a tray of takeaway coffees. His dark eyes flashed around the room as he placed them on the table.

"What's the news on Banks?" Scott asked, dropping a folder on the table. Drew handed him a coffee and several pages of notes.

"We just received a report from Donaldson's team," Drew said, sitting opposite Scott and looking at Michelle. "Michelle, give us an update."

"I trust everyone slept well," Michelle said, standing to direct everyone's attention to a map of St. Petersburg on the wall. Her thick black hair was neatly pinned at the back of her head. "Donaldson's team is checking all transport out of Moscow, but so far Banks hasn't been seen. She may still be hiding in Moscow or trying to cross the border in a private vehicle."

"Tell us about the Sheraton Palace Hotel," Drew said, reaching for his coffee mug.

"The team in Moscow found a room in the Sheraton where Banks was staying. She booked one night under the name of Mr. and Mrs. Robert and Diana Smith, paid in US dollars, with no passport record. At the time of check-in, Banks told staff that her husband was in a business meeting and had both their passports. There was no sign that anyone else had been in the room with her, but they did find a metro map for St. Petersburg and receipts from Kiev, confirming she had been here a few days ago and will probably return the same way."

"Anything else?" Scott asked.

"We did some checks in St. Petersburg, and found that she had also stayed one night in the Belmond Grand Hotel near Nevsky Prospect Metro and a second night in Nevsky Forum Hotel near the Mayakovskaya Metro. Same booking name, same story. There were several crosses on the metro map, meaning that she had been looking for something or somebody." Michelle paused. "We haven't found any links yet. That's all from Moscow."

Scott moved toward the centre of the room. "Marcus, I want you to continue tracking Banks' movements in Moscow and St. Petersburg. Drew, I want you and Jared watching the train station. Donaldson already has a team at the airport and along the main roads. Toni will be coordinating live camera feed and communications. Michelle, you and I will visit some local hotels."

The room was quiet.

"Okay people, I know it's been a long two days, but I don't have to tell you how important this is." He reached for his coffee and stood. "In this job, coffee is blood."

****

Six hours later, after returning to the hotel, Scott placed his fourth empty cup on the table. He was getting agitated. "Any news from the others?" he asked.

"Nothing yet," Toni replied, continuing to stare at the monitor in front of her.

Scott jumped to his feet. "I'm going back out. Michelle, you can stay here with Toni. Marcus and I will join the others at the station."

At the station, Scott positioned himself in front of a large screen displaying arrival and departure times. From there he scanned the hundreds of faces in the fast-moving crowd.

"Drew, where are you?" he said, testing his communicator.

"The bins on your left."

He turned and saw a man collecting bottles from a bin nearby. "Great work," he said, offering Drew a nod.

Half an hour later, Toni contacted the team. "Okay people! We have someone matching Banks' description approaching the main entrance. East side, two minutes away."

"Great news," Scott said, checking his watch. "Marcus, cover the main entrance. Let me know when you have a visual."

A short moment later, Marcus replied, "I've got a visual, but we have a problem."

"What's happening?"

"Target just stopped a taxi."

"Are you sure it's her?"

"Not 100 percent," Marcus replied.

Scott moved toward the entrance. "I'm on my way. Drew maintain position, she may try and backtrack to the station."

CHAPTER 19

Istanbul, Turkey

THE CALL TO PRAYER echoed through the streets as Susan adjusted her headscarf and stepped onto the footpath. Three days earlier, she had made a U-turn at the Ukrainian border and purchased a private flight from Kursk to Istanbul. Bribing border security wasn't a problem. Now, after hibernating for three days, she was eager to stretch her legs and explore the city. First on the list was a fake passport. Second, was clothes and new shoes. She had swapped her coat, headscarf, boots and handbag with another woman who was travelling to Kiev. The expensive fur coat was the deal clincher. Unfortunately, the other women's boots were half a size too small. As she looked up and down the street, a young boy ran up to her. His dark eyes sparkled.

"Paper for you, Miss?"

Susan looked at the young boy, surprised by how quickly he had appeared.

"I can't read Turkish."

The young boy turned to go. Susan stared at his bare feet and messy hair.

"Wait!"

She held up five dollars and the boys' eyes shone with excitement. "Can you show me this address?" She handed the boy an address on a small piece of notepaper. If you needed anything illegal, 'Those guys had it,' she had been promised.

"Yes, me know this street," the young boy said. His dark eyes fixed firmly on Susan.

The boy led her through the streets, looking back to make sure she was keeping up with him.

"What's your name?" Susan asked, as they stopped for traffic.

"Mohammed." The boy continued along the street. "America?"

"Yes, I'm American," Susan replied.

He turned and smiled.

"How old are you?" she asked.

"Ten," he said, straightening his body and holding up 10 fingers.

They continued until Mohammed stopped at a narrow alley. He held out his hand and Susan gave him the five-dollar note. The boy pointed down the dark alley.

"This is it?" Susan asked.

He nodded.

"Thank you, Mohammed. I hope I…."

"This is bad place," the boy said, interrupting her.

Before she could reply, he turned abruptly and disappeared among the crowds.

In the alley, a group of men walked out of a small doorway ahead of her. A young lady with blue jeans and an oversized t-shirt was being led behind. Susan looked into the woman's glassy eyes as the group passed her. She approached the small wooden door and turned to watch the group of men leave the alley. She hated the idea of doing business with people she didn't like, didn't trust, and had spent a big portion of her life trying to put behind bars, but desperation places you in situations that often demand compromise.

She whispered a short prayer and slowly turned the door handle. Inside, Susan's eyes slowly adjusted to the dim lit room. Groups of men sat against the walls smoking nargile pipes. Her lungs breathed the sweet-smelling tobacco that hung in the air, causing her to cough. She moved through the darkness and cringed at the thought of how many hideous crimes might have been previously planned there. After what seemed a lifetime, she finally reached a counter with words carved into the wooden surface. There were only two other women in the room, both sitting together with a group of backpackers.

A young man approached the counter and pushed his chin outward to form a question, saving himself the need to speak. Susan studied his beard and thick eyebrows.

"I need a passport," she said.

The young man looked at her with suspicion. The feeling was mutual. He walked through a curtain, leading into a backroom. A moment later, an older man moved the curtain back with one hand, looked at Susan, and vanished again. Susan waited patiently, using the opportunity to take a detailed look around the room. She was met by a wall of evil stares and turned around, preferring to look at the floral artwork on the wall behind the counter. After several minutes, a third man, middle aged, stepped from the back room.

"What you want?" he said, in a gruff tone.

"I need a passport."

The man studied her, taking a seat behind the counter. "Why you need passport?" he said, in his thick accent.

Susan decided to cut the small talk. "How much for a passport?" The man continued to stare. Susan didn't fit the profile of his regular customers. "1000 US," she said, hoping that the talk of money would move the conversation in a more positive direction.

"You want passport?"

Susan ignored his question. "How much?" She looked around nervously. "1500?"

The man remained silent and returned to the backroom again. Susan stared at the counter, looking out of the corner of her eyes at a group of people seated against a nearby wall. After an agonizing wait, one of the two young women she had passed on the way in, approached her.

"What are you after?" she asked, in a Boston accent.

Susan turned, pleased that someone in the room was willing to engage her in an intelligible conversation.

"Massachusetts?" Susan asked.

"Yes, that's where I grew up." She pointed in the direction of the second young woman who was still sitting. "My friend and I have been travelling the last three years."

"I've been travelling too. I ran into a bit of trouble in Russia and need a new identity."

"It happens," the young lady replied.

"I was told this was the place to come, but I'm not sure these guys want to help."

The young lady called toward the backroom. "Hassan?" The middle-aged man came out. "She won't cause trouble."

Susan looked across the counter, hopeful of success.

"8000," he said, before returning to the backroom.

The young lady moved close to Susan. "Don't give him more than 4000," she whispered.

The middle-aged man returned with the younger man, handing Susan a passport to inspect.

Susan examined the pages while the young lady held her mobile screen over the passport to add light. "Italian," Susan commented.

"They're good," the young lady said, "A friend used one a few weeks ago and had no problems."

Susan continued examining the pages. "2500."

The older man crossed his arms. "6000."

The young woman looked at Susan to offer support.

"3000," Susan said, holding a wad of notes on the counter.

"4000. Last offer."

"Give him half now and half on delivery," the young woman said, looking across the counter. Susan placed two rolls of cash on the counter, and the man counted the notes, stopping when he reached 1000, then continuing.

"Passport photo?"

Susan reached inside her bag and handed the man a photo.

"Come back Thursday," he said, turning abruptly and disappearing into the backroom.

Susan wiped her sweaty palms. "Thanks for the help," she said. "I'm Diane."

"No worries. I'm Jodie, but everyone calls me Jo."

"Can I trust these guys?"

Jo shook her head. "I don't trust anyone here, but don't worry, they sell good passports."

"Well, thanks again. Maybe I'll see you when I return."

"No problems. If you need any help, I'm staying at the Alliance Hostel."

Susan glanced around the room before slowly making her exit. As she left the building, the light of the alley caused her to squint. She took a deep breath and hurried from the alley. Her first black-market deal was in motion.

****

Back at the hotel, Susan approached the notice board. 'Increase Your Self Confidence. Self Defence Course. Tuesday Nights. Sophia Hotel. Call Juan.'

She wrote down the number and walked across to the reception desk. "Could you show me where the Sophia Hotel is?"

"It's just one street behind us," the receptionist said, pointing in the direction. "You're interested in the self-defence course?"

A look of surprise showed on her face. "Yes."

He smiled. "I'm Juan, the trainer. I work here as a second job."

"Wonderful!" Susan exclaimed. "Do you think I can learn?"

"Anyone can learn," he responded.

Susan looked him over. He certainly didn't fit her profile of a self defence expert. Thin, no bulging muscles. His gelled hair and expensive long-sleeved shirt made him appear more like a car salesman. "Do you also offer private lessons?"

"Yes, of course," he said. His face glowed with excitement. "I'm available tomorrow morning, if you like."

Carrying thousands of dollars around in her handbag was making Susan paranoid. If the lessons could help her self-confidence like the ad promised, it would be worth it.

"Tomorrow morning sounds perfect," she said.

Delta Bunker, Nevada Desert

"Scott, you're not going to believe this," Drew said.

"What is it?"

"We just got a match on Thomas Lansdowne." He paused for Scott's reaction.

"That's great news," Scott said. "Where is he?"

Drew remained silent.

"Well?"

"Nevada," Drew said, in a monotone voice.

The whole room was now looking in Scott's direction.

"Why does Lansdowne suddenly appear back in America after 10 years, and make a beeline for Nevada?" He held his chin, deep in thought. "Give me Cruse on the phone."

CHAPTER 20

Istanbul, Turkey

THE NEXT MORNING, Juan and Susan met in a small room in the Sophia Hotel. Juan had a very calming quality and Susan immediately felt comfortable in his presence.

"Maybe you can start by telling me why you want to learn?" Juan asked.

"Can you teach me what to do if I'm grabbed from behind?"

Juan laughed. "With a little practise, I can teach you to escape an attacker with a few simple moves."

"Really?"

"I'll teach you how to redirect an attacker's energy and strike the most vulnerable areas such as the eyes or groin."

Susan pressed her lips together.

Juan laughed again. "It sounds complicated, but you only need to learn a few simple moves, then it's just repetition."

Susan felt charmed by Juan's confidence in her. She knew the value of repetition. Every night before going to bed, she had made a nightly ritual of loading and unloading her small handgun. She had never fired it, but it no longer intimidated her.

Juan had Susan grab him from behind, and without warning, quickly broke free from her grip.

"By the end of this week, you'll be doing the same."

He demonstrated some moves and had Susan repeat them. After fifteen minutes, Susan stopped and took several deep breaths.

"Don't worry if it all seems a bit overwhelming," Juan said. "We'll be practising those same few moves every day until they become an automatic response."

Susan wiped her forehead with a small towel. She had always enjoyed pushing herself to new levels of endurance and skill.

"I feel so unfit."

"You're welcome to join me tomorrow for a morning jog," Juan suggested. "I can meet you in the lobby around 6am."

"That would be wonderful," Susan said, remembering her last jog with Kim in Columbia.

****

Susan shook as she washed her face. Ice cold water wasn't the most pleasant way to wake up, but unfortunately the hot water wasn't working. She changed clothes and met Juan in the lobby.

"Good morning, Susan. Are you ready for a nice run?"

"Let's take it slow this morning," she said, as they entered the street.

They jogged for several kilometres and arrived at the waterfront. A soft fog ascended off the ocean and the sound of seagulls filled the sky. At this hour of the day, Istanbul had a special mystic. Only a few people were out in the morning chill.

"Follow me," Juan said, climbing onto a small cement wall and lifting his body in a graceful motion to balance on the thin ledge. Susan joined him but fell after just a few seconds.

"You have to find your centre of balance," he said, helping her onto the wall to join him. "Bend your knees like this."

Susan fell to the ground again.

"Watch me," he said, walking effortlessly along the wall. "Try again."

Susan tried a third time, falling to the ground after a few steps.

"It's harder than it looks!" she said.

Juan stepped off the ledge and grabbed her hand. "Let's try it once more," he said, holding her hand for support. "Bend your knees, arms wide." Juan tapped gently on Susan's back. "Back straight, and eyes focused ahead."

Susan's legs stopped wobbling as she looked forward.

"That's right," Juan encouraged, releasing his grip on her hand.

Susan balanced perfectly.

"How am I doing?"

"Excellent! Keep your focus on an object in front of you."

"There's a ribbon hanging from a tree," she replied.

Juan stood a small distance away. "That's great. Stay focused and step toward the ribbon."

"I don't think I can." Susan said, looking down. She took a step and lost balance, landing on the ground.

"What just happened?"

"I lost my balance," Susan said, laughing at herself.

Juan smiled. "And how did that happen?"

"I lost my focus, didn't I?"

Juan helped her into position again. "Let's try once more."

Susan stood on top of the small ledge, wobbling for a few seconds.

"How's your back?" Juan asked.

Susan immediately straightened her body.

"Now, tell me about the ribbon?"

"What do you mean?" she asked.

"Describe the ribbon."

"It has stripes."

"What else?"

"It's a red colour."

"That's great. Now take a step, and tell me where the ribbon is hanging?"

"Two metres from the ground on the left side of the tree."

"Take another step and tell me what it's made of."

"It looks plastic," she said, taking another step forward.

"Excellent!"

Susan looked around and jumped off.

"Wow! I made it!"

Juan laughed.

"Thanks so much," Susan said.

Juan placed his hand on her shoulder. "You did the walking. I just helped you stay focused on walking, instead of falling. We can practise again tomorrow, until you can walk along the whole ledge."

****

The following day, Susan lay in bed listening to the call to prayer outside her window. She reached for her small bible, flipping through the pages at the back and reading a verse from the help section.

'Don't be full of fear. I am with you.' The words 'I am with you', ran through her mind as she prepared herself for jogging.

A half hour later, she met Juan. They ran for several kilometres, stopping near the Galata bridge to stretch their muscles.

"How did you end up in Istanbul?" Susan asked.

"I grew up in Barcelona. Married a local girl. Life was really happy, but after three years the marriage fell apart."

"I'm sorry to hear that."

"It was a sad time in my life." He paused. "I travelled around Italy, then Greece, and finally Turkey. After a few months, I ran out of money and found work here." He laughed. "You were probably expecting a more interesting reason."

"I can relate to unexpected events changing the direction of your life," Susan said. "My husband died a few years ago, and I've been travelling ever since."

Juan pointed at the wall. "Let's see how you do today," he said, deliberately changing the topic.

Susan leapt onto the wall with her arms outstretched. Within a few seconds she had control of her balance.

"How's our ribbon looking today?" Juan asked, creating a playful mood.

"It's looking good," she said, taking a step forward.

Juan stood observing Susan as she took one step in front of the other. As she approached the half way point, he moved closer to encourage her.

"Great work. You're half way."

Susan remained focused, taking one step after another.

"Keep it up. You're almost there. Six more steps!"

Susan wobbled.

"Five more steps. Three more!"

Susan took the last step and leapt in the air. "Woohoo!" she yelled, spinning around and giving Juan a high five.

"Well done! Yesterday that wall seemed such a big obstacle."

Susan nodded.

"But you faced the challenge and achieved your goal. What can you learn from this experience?"

"I achieved my goal much quicker than I expected," she said.

"Exactly! You achieved your goal in a fraction of the time that you thought it would take."

Susan smiled proudly.

"Most people underestimate their abilities," Juan said, looking into Susan's eyes to reinforce his point. "Susan, you can do anything you set your mind on."

"Thanks for reminding me," she said.

****

Later that day, Susan returned to the small club to collect her passport. The mood of the place was very different today. The room was filled with women, glazed expressions, medicated and barely conscious. She walked to the counter and felt the leering stares from several men nearby. The middle-aged man, alerted to Susan's presence, immediately appeared from the back room and presented her with a passport. Susan flipped through the pages, scrutinizing the binding and print quality.

"Blank original," the man said.

Susan placed two rolls of cash on the counter. The man removed several rubber bands, and she watched as he counted each note.

"4500," he said, looking up at Susan and flipping the last few notes through his fingers.

"We agreed on 4000," Susan replied, staring him in the eyes. After what seemed a lifetime, she called his bluff by turning and walking to the door. Her stomach churned inside. As the door closed behind her, Susan took a deep breath and continued walking. Her heart beat wildly. At the end of the alley, she turned to check if anyone was following. After walking to the end of the block, she opened the passport and looked at the identification page. "Maria Amorosi, Milan, Italy." Susan took another deep breath, and stepping onto the road, she waved a taxi. This was an event that needed celebrating. She was returning to America.

CHAPTER 21

C RUSE REPLAYED THE recording. "Hello Mr. Cruse. This is Susan Banks. I have the Flashlight list."

"It's definitely Banks' voice," Eric said. "We compared the recording to archived phone records and got a perfect match."

Cruse's eyebrows furrowed. "Any idea of location?" he asked.

"We traced the number to a public phone box in Kansas City," Eric replied. "We have a team searching the area, but no news yet."

"Surveillance cameras?"

Eric shook his head. "We've checked all street cameras in the area. It's like she was invisible. The whole surveillance team is baffled."

"How does a lawyer's assistant manage to travel around the world, evading every attempt to track her down?" Cruse asked, pacing back and forward across the room. "Now she's in our own backyard and she is still one step ahead of us." He slammed a file on the desk. "Give me Scott on the line."

"Yes, Sir."

Eric dialled Scott's number and stood quietly to one side. This was one phone call he didn't want to miss. He had been working as Cruse's assistant for three years and had seen Cruse at both his best and worst. So far, he had managed to escape Cruse's worst, but calls like this were a good reminder for him.

A few moments later, Scott answered.

"Scott here. What's up?"

Around the operations room, all faces were turned in Scott's direction. Cruse never rang unless someone's butt was about to fry.

Cruse raised his voice. "What do you mean, what's up?" He paused. "We have Susan Banks calling CIA headquarters, and you guys probably haven't realised she's in the country."

"Susan Banks?" Scott stared at the others before walking off to his office for privacy. "What did she say?" Scott asked, shaking his head.

"She says she has the Flashlight list. Damn it, Scott! What's going on?"

"We've been monitoring her lawyer friends, so if she tries making contact, we'll have her," Scott replied. "Do we have a location for the call?"

Cruse waved Eric over.

"The call was made from a public phone in Kansas City. Eric will send through the details."

Eric nodded and disappeared out the door.

Cruse cleared his throat. "My guess is that she wants to make a deal."

Scott grunted his agreement.

"When she makes contact again, I want your guys in the phone booth with her."

Scott brushed his hair back in frustration.

"It's our turn to be one step ahead of her; and Lansdowne, who knows what he's up to."

"They will be working together, so if we can track one of them, we will have the other," Scott said, unsure of anything he was saying.

"Scott, if this gets out of hand; you know we're all going down. If you need more resources," he paused, "Banks is our top priority. Finish this."

CHAPTER 22

Unknown location, Nevada

THE BLANK WALLS were partially lit by a small light in one of the corners above the door. In the opposite corner, a camera monitored her movement. Her lips moved in silent prayer. Weeks of being blindfolded, transported via cars and planes, and kept in solitude, had caused the occupant to reach a point of delirium. Suddenly, the door clicked open and a large man in military uniform stood in the doorway, silhouetted by the bright light behind him.

"On your feet!"

"Where am I?"

He ignored her question, cuffing her wrists, then jabbing her arm with a needle. They walked through a long hallway, stopping at a check point. The man waved his wrist bracelet over a scanner, registering his departure. He waved a second bracelet past the scanner and fastened it to his prisoner's right arm. The woman's eyes became more alert as the injection took effect. He led her along another hallway and they passed several enormous glass windows. People in white overalls were working at tables with large microscopes.

"This way," he said.

They continued down the corridor and stopped outside a small room. He guided her through the door.

"Someone will be with you shortly."

The door closed behind her. Soft blue light reflected off the walls. Much more pleasant than her tiny room. In the centre of the room, there was a small table and three chairs. One of the walls featured a mirrored window. She took a seat and looked down at the table.

After several minutes, two people entered the room. The more senior man placed a folder on the table.

"Kim Knox."

Kim looked up, staring into his eyes.

"You have an interesting story," he said, opening his file. "Do you recognise this man?"

"Of course!" Kim replied, snatching the photo from his hand.

"Would you like to see him today?" His voice was calm and purposeful.

Kim's face was emotionless. "Alfred is dead."

"We have Alfred here with us," the man said. "Answer a few questions, and we'll take you to see him."

Tears rolled from Kim's eyes. "What do you want to know?"

The two men exchanged glances, pleased with how the interview was proceeding.

The senior man continued. "You left your home and children in America after being in police custody. Why?"

"I didn't feel safe."

"Who gave you the idea that you weren't safe?"

He thumbed through several other pages in his file, before staring back at Kim.

"Charlie." Kim paused. "Charlie told us we weren't safe and we had to leave."

Kim looked back and forth between the two men. She didn't trust them, but felt safe to share, since she had no information on Charlie's location.

"Who is Charlie?"

"Tom's uncle."

"Tom Banks?"

Kim nodded and the younger man wrote in his notepad.

"So, this Charlie told you it was unsafe to stay in America, and then arranged for you to leave the country?"

Kim nodded again.

"You also visited Paris," he said, leaning back in his chair. "What were you doing in Paris, and how did you get there?"

Kim sat silent for a few seconds, quickly scanning her brain. She had no idea if Thomas or Susan were still alive, and certainly didn't want to offer information that would place them in danger. On the other hand, if Susan was being held prisoner in the same facility, their stories needed to match; otherwise she may not be able to see Alfred.

"How do I know that you're telling the truth about Alfred?" Kim asked, changing the topic.

The two men looked at each other and stood to exit the room. The old man stopped in the doorway, looking back at Kim.

"We'll be right back."

Kim used the time to think through her responses to any further questions. She decided that she would not continue answering questions until they gave her proof that Alfred was alive. Her heart beat faster as she considered the possibility.

The older man returned a moment later, with two men in military uniform. He moved close and unlocked the handcuffs from her wrists, smiling to communicate a gesture of goodwill.

"My name is Harry," he said, then turned and walked to the door. "Follow me."

Kim froze, unsure of what was happening. Harry turned and waved his hand with a pleasant smile. One of the two uniformed soldiers directed her out of the room. Harry's grey and slightly balding head moved steadily along the corridor in front of her. After several minutes, he stopped in the doorway of a large room with monitors. Two heads peered through the doorway to look at Kim. Harry carried a certain degree of authority, and if Alfred was still alive, Kim felt confident that he could authorize a visit. They moved along the corridor and stepped into a lift. Everything was glossy white and not a spot of dust. Alfred would feel at home. The lift slid open and the two men escorted Kim across a hall into a wide viewing platform. The domed-shaped platform stood about ten metres above the floor below. At least fifty people in white lab coats were working below.

Harry turned toward Kim. "This is our main laboratory. It's completely enclosed by glass to ensure a dust-free environment."

Kim looked down at the high-tech bracelet on her wrist. Apart from the bracelet, she might have even felt like a tourist.

"Is Alfred here?" she asked.

"He's working in another section. We're heading there now."

Harry gave her a reassuring smile as they continued walking around the glass perimeter that circled high above the laboratory. Kim's eyes scanned the people below. One of the men in lab coats looked up, and for a brief moment their eyes connected. Suddenly, they entered a room, and Kim was led to a black leather couch. She had not been in a room of such luxury since her abduction at the palace. The men left her on the couch and disappeared before she could ask questions. After several minutes of studying the room's marbled tiles, she approached the door and pressed the entry button. The door opened in a quick silent motion. Kim peeked outside. The corridor was empty. She looked down at the bracelet on her wrist. There was no use trying to run, the bracelet would track her movement. The door automatically closed and she walked toward the large window at the back of the room. One of the men was assembling some type of handgun, while several others were gathered around a small flying object. Kim returned to the couch. Her palms were now sweating with anticipation.

Suddenly, the door opened and Alfred walked in. Kim leapt to her feet, and Alfred rushed forward to meet her in a passionate embrace.

"I thought you were dead," Kim said, with tears running down her cheeks.

Alfred squeezed Kim tight. "It's okay, Baby. It's going to be okay."

He wiped the tears from Kim's face with the back of his hand, while Harry and his assistant left the room.

"How long have you been here?

"A few days, I think," Kim replied, crying from happiness.

Alfred held Kim's face between his hands. "It's so great to see you, Darling." He gave her a gentle kiss and they stared in disbelief into each other's eyes.

"You're alive," she repeated.

Alfred wiped Kim's tears again, and they sat on the couch holding each.

"How are the children?" Alfred asked.

"I think they're still with Lynne." Kim's mouth quivered. "I haven't seen them in over eighteen months."

Alfred burst into tears, and squeezed her again. Ten minutes later, the door slid open.

"I'm glad you've had a chance to reunite," Harry said. "Unfortunately, we all have work, so for now I'll need to separate you." His voice carried a sympathetic tone.

Kim and Alfred stared at each other.

"Everything will work out, Honey," Alfred said, fighting off tears as he was led out the door.

Harry nodded, acknowledging Alfred's cooperation. Back in the interviewing room, Kim took a seat and waited for Harry to reappear. The younger man was already in the room with his recorder.

"I need a drink," Kim said, still wiping tears from her eyes.

"Of course," the young man said, walking from the room.

Kim looked at the door, then turned her face toward the table, wondering what she would say about the trip to Paris, Raheem, Thomas, and Susan. She was already regretting the mention of Charlie. In here, there were none of the legal protocols one might expect. Everything was off the record, at least any traceable record.

A little while later, the two men returned. A young lady also accompanied them, offering Kim a glass of water and tissues, then leaving. Kim sipped the water.

"When will I see Alfred again?"

"Let's see how well we do with the interview before deciding that," Harry said, asserting his authority. He turned over a few pages in his file. "Let's start with Mr. Raheem Ahmad." His lips tightened. "What can you tell us?"

"I met Mr. Ahmad in Casablanca." Kim studied Harry's large ears and double chin. "He offered me a place to stay."

"And were you travelling with anyone?"

"No, I was alone."

Harry pushed a photo in front of Kim. "Do you recognise this photo?"

Kim forced a smile. "I can't recall having my photo taken."

"This was taken by a security camera at the Concorde Metro, in Paris." Harry stared at her without showing emotion. "The person with you is Susan Banks. We are very interested in knowing where she is." He paused. "And we will find out, one way or another." He pushed another photo in front of Kim. "Have you ever seen this man?"

Kim touched the photo. "No." she replied, pushing the photo away.

"His name is Thomas Lansdowne. He's wanted on charges of espionage and treason."

The room went silent as Harry sat thinking. The young man taking notes finally broke the silence.

"What can you tell us about Flashlight?"

"I don't understand," Kim said, using a monotone voice.

Harry leaned forward over the table. "You accessed a deposit box in Paris. Tell us about it." He turned to look at his assistant.

Kim sat in silence, realizing that the less she said, the better.

"Mrs. Knox, if you want to play games." He paused. "Let me assure you, we can play games too; and you want to be careful, because when we play." Harry's tone became threatening as he emphasized his last statement. "Someone. Will. Get hurt." He closed his file and stood abruptly. "We're done for today," he said, biting his bottom lip. He faced his assistant at the door. "When Mrs. Knox is ready to see her husband again, we will continue the interview." He looked back at Kim and left the room. The young man followed him out, leaving Kim alone.

Kim wept. Things had now changed. Knowing that Alfred was alive, but unable to see him, was a greater torture than believing he was dead. She looked at the door. Every desire inside was screaming to run. She sat waiting to be led back to her cell, making a mental note of the cameras in the room. A minute later, the door opened and a young man in uniform approached her with handcuffs. Kim ignored him and headed straight into the corridor. The young soldier chose to ignore her act of defiance, returning the handcuffs to his belt and leading Kim back to her cell. As Kim walked back to her cell, she smiled. They were looking for Susan, and that meant that Susan was still alive… somewhere.

CHAPTER 23

A YOUNG LADY PLACED a large cup on Cruse's desk. "Sir, your coffee."

Cruse looked up to acknowledge her and held his hand over the mouthpiece of his phone. "Thanks Sarah." She smiled and left the room. "I'll get back to you later today," he said, resuming his conversation. "No, there won't be any further delays." He sat back in his chair. "You'll have it on your desk today. I'll call you back."

Cruse placed the phone on his table and sat in silence. Berkley was a necessary evil in his world of corrupt business dealings, but he held the budget strings, and that made him an important asset. Cruses' thoughts were interrupted by Eric.

"Sir, we have a development. You need to see this."

Cruse looked startled. "What's happening?"

"Susan Banks just made contact again."

Cruse jumped to his feet, following Eric down the hallway to the communications room. His day had just been rescheduled. As they entered the room, Eric signalled the communications manager to replay the message.

"We received this call two minutes ago. It's a positive match to Banks."

The message was played. "Robert Cruse, meet me at Starbucks in 40 minutes. Come alone."

"Location?"

"Langley, Sir," Eric replied. "She's here in Langley."

"Phone Scott."

Eric wasted no time, picking up a nearby phone. Cruse walked back to his office deep in thought. By the time he returned the phone was ringing.

"Any news on Banks?" he asked.

"We have our eyes on the ground, but nothing yet," Scott replied.

"Susan Banks just visited Langley to invite me for a coffee." Cruse's voice caused Scott to panic and he rubbed his eyebrows.

"I can be there in four hours," Scott said.

"Our coffee meeting is scheduled in…" Cruse looked at his watch. "Thirty-two minutes."

"Did she say anything else?"

"No, nothing," Cruse said, holding back his temper. "How far along are we with Flashlight?"

"Phase one is complete, and we're only a week away from completing phase two."

Scott was puzzled by Cruse's sudden change in topic.

"Okay, keep pushing phase two. I'll deal with Banks."

Cruse ended the call, leaving Scott staring at the wall. Banks was one problem he was glad to pass onto Cruise.

Delta Bunker, Nevada Desert

"Scott, you might want to take a look at this," Greg said, stepping into Scott's office.

"What now?" Scott said, annoyed at the timing.

"We have a group of protestors at the main gate."

"Have them arrested. There are more important things on my mind right now."

"All 2000 of them?" Greg replied.

Scott looked up. "Who are they, and why wasn't I informed earlier?" Scott asked, with a puzzled expression.

"They appear to be anti-war demonstrators," Greg replied.

"What do you mean?" Scott said. "Don't we have informers in these groups?"

"It seems to be linked to a viral internet campaign," Greg said.

"Okay, but first we have another problem."

"Banks?" Greg asked, looking down at his wrist.

Scott looked up.

Greg touched his wrist band. "Just received a message from the surveillance team." He raised his eyebrows. "Banks is in Langley?"

Scott nodded. "She's arranged a meeting with Cruse at Starbucks in the next half an hour, and hopefully it's the last we hear of her."

"Cruse ordered a hit on her?"

Scott nodded. "We just have Thomas Lansdowne to deal with." He held his chin. "Run a search on all Lansdowne's relatives. It's time we created some pain."

Greg was shocked by the callousness in Scott's voice. He left the room rubbing his forehead.

Starbucks, Langley, Virginia

Susan entered the building and glanced sideways to examine her new appearance in a mirrored wall panel. Short red hair, a white blouse, black skirt and high heels. She placed an order and sat against the back wall of Starbucks, next to the toilets. She looked at the main door for any sign of Cruse.

"Though I walk through the valley. You are with me," she whispered.

Her eyes scanned the room, stopping to focus on a young man with a Smartphone. A minute later, an older man in his mid-sixties entered. Susan took a deep breath as he walked toward her.

"Hello, Susan," Cruse said, removing his large coat.

"Mr. Robert Cruse."

"That's right."

He sat opposite her and Susan studied the wrinkles on his face. He looked like he had lived a stressful life.

"I understand you have something for me," he said, getting directly to the point.

Susan laughed. "You have a cheek," she said, mustering up all her courage to continue. "You walk in here, with that smug look on your face, thinking that I'm just going to hand over your precious information." She paused. Her eyes penetrating his eyes. Cruse sat silent. "You arranged the death of my husband Tom, and I want answers!"

Cruse refused to flinch. "Susan, I am truly sorry for your loss, but I'm not responsible for your husband's death." He paused. "The whole Alfred Knox affair is a tragedy, but the men responsible are now behind bars." He continued his stare. "My job…" He paused. "Our job; is to serve this nation and provide a safer world for everyone." He forced a smile.

Susan moved her legs uncomfortably. "If the men responsible for Tom's death are in prison, then who on earth has been threatening my life for the last two years?"

Cruse leaned back in his chair. "You can try and pass the blame, but I can't help anyone who is working against me."

"How am I working against you?"

"We believe you have information that is considered to be sensitive to our national security," Cruse replied. "If you are willing to cooperate and surrender the flash drive, I would be more than happy to arrange for someone to investigate your concerns of personal safety."

Susan's head dropped toward the table. "My good friend Kim Knox is missing." She stood. "And I believe you know where she is. If you want your flash drive, I need to know that Kim is alive." She signalled the waitress. Cruse remained seated, looking at Susan. "Mr. Cruse will have a toasted coffee, while I visit the lady's room," she said, quickly vanishing around the corner. The waitress looked at Cruse. Cruse dismissed the waitress and signalled his two field agents to follow Susan.

The two agents entered the female toilets, but only found a young mother and her child. They hurried into the male toilets, but Susan had vanished. They searched a second time before returning to Cruse.

"She's gone!"

Cruse thumped his fist on the table. "Impossible!" He shook his head. "Damn it!"

The waitress looked around, startled.

"What the hell just happened?" Cruse asked, addressing his team who were listening in.

"We had cameras on everybody," Eric said, speaking through Cruse's earpiece. "We even placed a camera on the waitress!"

"Lockdown the building and establish a two-block perimeter. She can't just disappear!" He shook his head. "This woman has all our heads on the chopping board, so let's not stuff this up. She's not an alien from outer space. She's got to be here somewhere."

Cruse's agents secured all entrances in and out of the building, and several minutes later, two officers with sniffer dogs arrived. Cruse walked into the toilets to look around. Not a single trace. One of the officers with a dog entered behind him.

"This is where she was last seen?" the officer asked.

"This is the last place she wasn't seen," Cruse said, rubbing his forehead. The dog sniffed around the room, while Cruse examined the ceiling.

"Check those ceiling panels."

One of his agents balanced on top of a hand basin, hitting the ceiling to remove several panels. He poked his head into the ceiling, and held a small torch in front of him.

"See anything?"

"Nothing yet, Sir."

Cruse stepped into the hall. "We need a spotlight!"

After a few minutes, someone came running with a large torch. Cruse pointed to the door opposite. "Check inside the ceiling of the male toilets."

He returned to the female toilets, deep in thought. He had seen Banks come in here with his own eyes. A phone call broke his train of thought.

"Eric. What have you got?" He closed the lid on a toilet and sat down.

"I'm sorry Sir, we've got nothing here. We've replayed the video feed a dozen times. She enters the toilets and just disappears."

"Magnificent," Cruse said, with a sarcastic tone. "We train our agents to be shadows, and this woman makes us all look like class clowns."

"We will find her," Eric said. "She's not a ghost."

Cruse stared at the toilet. "If this goes pear shaped, we're all in the shithouse."

CHAPTER 24

New York

L OOKS LIKE WE might be in for some heavy snow," said the Taxi driver. "Coming home from holidays?"

"Yes, a two-year holiday."

The taxi driver looked in his mirror. "That's one hell of a holiday, Lady."

Susan laughed. His choice of words was painfully true. After twenty minutes, they arrived at a small hotel.

"Stay warm," the driver said, turning to smile, "And don't work too hard. It's bad for your health." He coughed loudly, as if to confirm his point.

Susan waved. It felt good being back among New Yorkers. Inside her room, she replayed the recording of her meeting at Starbucks. There was no incriminating evidence to point the finger at Cruse.

"A big fat fail," she said, flopping on the bed.

A few hours later, as Susan entered the lobby, everyone was talking about the wild weather. The snow and cold wind blasted her face as she stepped outside. She pulled her scarf up around her mouth and nose. The concierge waved down a taxi. On a day like today, she didn't envy his job. Looking out of the taxi,

Susan watched the snow fly past. New York was in for a turbulent day.

The taxi stopped several blocks down the road. At least today, the snow would provide a blanket of protection from street cameras. She made her way into a large building and turned to enter a small coffee shop with décor from the 1940's. A waitress directed her to a secluded spot in the corner. Susan sat admiring the chandelier in the centre of the room and several minutes later, Graham arrived. He carried a small laptop case over his shoulder, and a folder in his opposite hand.

"Susan, how are you?"

Susan stood to give him a hug.

"I see you've changed your hair style," he said, placing his bag on the floor.

"You like the short black fringe?"

Graham nodded his approval and turned to the waitress. "A cappuccino please." He turned to face Susan.

"I'll have the same."

As the waitress left, Graham was interrupted by a call on his phone.

"Hi Paul. Yes, but can we make it 10:30? I'm with an old friend." He looked up at Susan, waiting for the reply. "That's great. See you then."

Graham was the typical multitasker, lots of activity, but poor at organization.

"I was sorry to hear about Tom."

"That's partly why I'm here, Graham. I need your help." Susan pushed a small recorder towards him. He immediately pressed the button to begin playback.

"Who is this?" He said, adjusting his glasses, with curiosity showing on his face.

"Robert Cruse, CIA's Deputy Director of the NCS."

"And what are we listening to here?" Graham asked, keen to waste no time.

"I have good reason to believe that he was responsible for Tom's death."

Graham moved back in his chair. "Whoa! Susan. You're standing on shaky ground." He stared into her face. "That's a big accusation."

The waitress returned, placing two cups on the table. "Two cappuccinos."

Susan reached for her cup and leaned forward. "Cruse is in charge of a program creating top secret military weapons. I believe it's being managed by the Science and Technology Division." Susan handed him an A4 sheet of paper. "Tom got in the way and was killed, along with many others."

Graham looked at the page shaking his head with disappointment.

"For crying out loud, Susan. This is an organisational chart from the internet, of all places." He pursed his lips together. "If you're going to make claims of murder against anyone, you need hard evidence, a quality recording, photos, phone records or something useful." He handed the recorder and paper back to her. "My editor would laugh if I showed him this… and you of all people should know the legal system." He shook his head to emphasize his last point.

"I realise I don't have the evidence. I'm not asking you to publish a story. I just want you to ask around, make a few inquiries, and see what you can find out." She pushed several photos across the table.

"Look I can't make any promises," he said, staring at the photos. "What are these?"

"2000 protesters in the Nevada Desert."

"No way! Are they all wearing Anonymous masks?"

Susan smiled. "Yes, and they're setting up a tent city, with plans to stay a while."

"Okay, this is a story I can run with."

He flicked through the photos again, glancing up at Susan. "Where did you get these pictures?"

She smiled. "I have friends in the desert."

"Look, I can't promise anything, but I have a friend with CIA contacts."

He glanced at the photos again. "Can I keep these?"

"Yes, of course. Just make a few inquiries for me, and in the meantime, I'll get some hard evidence."

"Give me a week and I'll ask around," he said, changing his tone to show appreciation for the photos.

****

Back in her hotel, and glad to be sheltered from the wind outside, Susan placed her handbag on the bed and saw a note on the table.

"Corner of North Jackson Road and Arlington Boulevard, 7:00pm, tomorrow night."

Arlington was only 20 minutes from Langley. The note was asking her to return to the lion's den. She checked the bathroom for intruders. Heading back to Langley wasn't on her to-do list, but she trusted the note.

CHAPTER 25

CIA Headquarters, Langley, Virginia

"YOUR COFFEE, SIR."

Cruse stared at the cup on his desk. The sight of coffee created a knot in his stomach. Susan Banks' disappearance the previous day was still fresh on his mind. He picked up his phone and dialled Scott's number.

"Scott, any news on Thomas Lansdowne?"

Berkley was already making his life miserable and he wanted to eliminate the possibility of any further slipups.

"We're working on Lansdowne's relatives. Everyone he knows is under 24-hour surveillance," Scott replied.

Cruse's fingers tapped the desk. "Great. We haven't got time to chase ghosts. Let's finish this."

"I understand, Sir," Scott replied, masking his wounded confidence.

"Keep me in the loop and send any progress reports to Eric."

Cruse ended the call just as Eric entered the room.

"We have an update on Starbucks."

Cruse braced himself.

"We know how she disappeared," Eric said, straightening his shoulders.

"This, I'm keen to see." Cruse leapt from his chair. "Sarah, bring my coffee to the meeting room."

As Cruse entered the room, a wall monitor displayed images of Susan. Eric cued his team and several more images appeared on the screen.

Eric pointed to the monitor. "This is a sales contract for Starbucks. A Mr. Bruce Reynold purchased the business just a few months ago."

"August," Cruse said, noting the contract date.

"Yes, but this is where it gets interesting." He pointed to the screen which now displayed a set of building plans. "This is a copy of the original plans, used for the building in 2003." He looked across at Cruse.

"And the point?"

"Oh, this is good, believe me," Eric said. "A few months ago, the building was partly closed for..." He paused to emphasize his next point. "Bathroom renovations." Eric looked at Cruse. "We called in some guys and pulled both bathrooms apart, piece by piece, until we discovered this." He pointed at another image on the screen.

"What are we looking at here?" Cruse asked.

"The men's bathroom has been duplicated."

Cruse's face wrinkled.

Eric continued, "Banks went inside the men's bathroom, and remotely triggered a mechanical process to swap the bathrooms. Our guys walked into the women's bathroom, realised she wasn't there, giving Banks just enough time to make the swap."

Cruse shook his head. "Ingenious! So, she was working with whoever renovated the bathrooms."

"Apparently, but we're still working on the connection." Eric pointed at the monitor. "We do know that after she made the swap, she was able to exit through the underground car park, where she had a hire car waiting."

"Are you saying we had no one watching the car park?"

Eric pressed his lips together.

"Damn it!" Cruse jumped to his feet. "We've been chasing Banks around the world for the last two years, and she escapes in a damn hire car!"

CHAPTER 26

Arlington, Virginia

A BLACK LIMO stopped alongside Susan, and the electric window lowered.

"Miss Banks?"

Susan's heart fluttered with apprehension. Stepping into a stranger's car was anti intuitive, but she trusted the note. Sometimes you just need to take a leap of faith and hope for a soft landing.

As they drove, Susan stared into the sky, thinking of the palace balcony and Raheem. She looked down at the note, wondering if Raheem had organised tonight's meeting. In truth, she had no idea if he was even alive. She leaned toward the mirror to check her appearance. The red evening dress and black fur coat were a last-minute purchase before leaving New York. She pressed the intercom, looking through at the driver.

"I hope I'm dressed appropriately?"

The driver checked his mirror. "You look fine, Madam."

"Typical male response," Susan whispered.

Gazing out the window again, she prayed. "The Lord is my shepherd."

CIA Headquarters, Langley, Virginia

"Your car is ready," Sarah said.

Cruse grabbed his coat, preparing to leave his office. He had an important dinner meeting at his favourite restaurant. Eric met him in the hallway while waiting for the elevator.

"Any news on the mystery owner of Starbucks?"

"Nothing yet," Eric said, holding his hand up to cover a yawn.

"Massive day for everyone," Cruse replied. "You did well."

It was a rare day indeed when Cruse gave anyone compliments. Eric savoured the moment.

"Thanks." Eric replied.

A black Cadillac was waiting as Cruse and Eric stepped from the elevator and parted company. Moments later, the Cadillac made its way through the streets.

"Care to listen to some music, Sir?" the driver asked.

Cruse looked up, interrupted from his thoughts. "Yes, something classical." He studied the driver. "You're new here."

"Yes, Sir. My first day."

The young African-American had been recruited a year before, and had just finished his initial training.

"Well son, I hope you enjoy working with us. What's your name?"

The young man looked at his mirror with a big toothy smile. "Alvin, Sir."

Cruse was thinking about the previous day as the car stopped at traffic lights.

"Never underestimate your enemy," he said aloud.

Alvin looked in the mirror. "I'm sorry. Never what?"

"Alvin, there's one thing I've learned in this game." He looked directly into the mirror. "Never underestimate your enemy."

Alvin's eyes moved back and forth, between the mirror and the road. "Yes, Sir. I'll remember that."

Cruse had worked hard for his current position. He had left college early to join the army and served in Vietnam, working his way up through the ranks until the CIA recruited him. After doing enough favours for the right people, and staying out of trouble, he was eventually promoted as Deputy Director of the NCS division (National Clandestine Service). He stared out the window wearily; looking forward to the day he would kiss the CIA goodbye, and pursue his own goals.

"Alvin, where are we heading?"

"Pimmit Hills, Sir," he said, confidently.

Cruse sat upright in the back. "Who told you Pimmit Hills?"

Alvin started to stammer. "I… I… get messages here; on this screen," he said, clearly shocked by the apparent misunderstanding.

"Turn the car around now!"

Alvin's head was spinning. A mistake on the first day was certainly an omen of doom. He pulled the car over to the side of the road. His heart rate doubled.

"Where to?" he asked, keeping his eyes focused on the road.

"Ultimatum Resta…" Cruse was interrupted by the sudden appearance of gas fumes. He reached for the door handle.

"Open the door! Open the door!"

Alvin pressed the door controls several times, coughing, until he finally slumped over the steering wheel unconscious.

Elm Street, McLean, Virginia

Susan's limousine came to an abrupt stop outside a plain office building.

"This way," the driver said, leading her up to a side entrance and pressing a door button. A few seconds later, a young lady with long blond hair opened the door.

"My name is Julianne. I'll be your host for the night." She took Susan's coat and directed her inside to a fine dining restaurant. "I'll be just a moment. Please take a seat and I'll bring you a drink."

Susan looked around the room. The building's plain outside appearance, was a stark contrast to the beautiful décor inside. She sat back in her chair, relaxed in part by the jazz music playing in the background. A few moments later, Julianne appeared with a glass of juice.

"Pineapple, orange and cranberry," she said, placing the glass on the table. Susan's mouth dropped open. Whoever was organising this, had done their homework. The hostess vanished before she could ask questions. Susan watched as more guests started filling the room and a few minutes later, Julianne returned.

"I'm sure you have a lot of questions, but everything will start to make sense in the next few minutes."

"Who invited me here?"

"You mean the note?"

"Yes." Susan held up the note.

Julianne laughed. "That's my handwriting. Come." She motioned Susan to follow her into a back room. "We'll be able to hear and see everything that happens tonight through this one-way mirror."

Susan shook her head. "I'm still lost. What's happening?"

"Stay here and keep watching. I don't want to spoil the surprise. I'll come and get you when we're ready." She smiled, then left the room.

Inside the hidden room, Susan watched with interest as two men carried a body into the restaurant, and positioned it at a table outside her window. She moved closer.

"Robert Cruse!"

One of the staff leaned under the table. "Table microphone activated," he said. He stood and took a few steps backward. "Testing, one, two, three."

"We hear you loud and clear, Jamie," another man replied.

Susan was observing everything from the hidden room, when suddenly, Cruse started to move.

"Okay. Take your positions," Julianne said, her voice transmitting through the sound system in Susan's room.

Another young hostess leaned across the table, tapping Cruse on the shoulder. "Mr. Cruse?"

Cruse looked around, recognizing the restaurant, and checked his Rolex watch. "What happened?"

"You just fell asleep for a few minutes," she replied.

Cruse yawned. "Have I eaten?" he asked, still feeling dazed from his unplanned nap.

"No. You're early for a dinner meeting. We had a booking for three." She placed a glass of water on the table. "You missed a call a few moments ago."

Cruse removed his cell phone, staring at the number on the screen. It was Scott.

"Would you like anything else while you're waiting?" she asked.

"I'm fine," Cruse replied, staring at his phone and calling Scott.

Delta Bunker, Nevada Desert

Scott's assistant Greg walked through the hallways of the underground bunker, deep in thought. He had been living underground for the last four years. Three of those years had been spent hoping for a transfer. There must be more to life than staring at monitors underground, he thought. As he walked towards the canteen, he wondered how much more he could take.

"What's it tonight, Greg?" Rex, the canteen manager asked.

"Same as usual," Greg replied. "Meat, mashed potato, carrots and peas." It was what he was brought up on.

"You look like you could use a holiday."

Greg laughed. "This place starts to get to your head after not seeing enough sun." His head dropped, realising the truth in what he had just said.

"It's probably better than working in the mines," Rex replied.

"I guess it could be worse."

As Greg sat alone eating, he thought of Kim Knox. Here was a woman in solitary confinement, forced to leave her two children, deprived of seeing her husband, and yet she seemed able to create her own joy. He had stared at the monitors, studying her day after day, and often listening to her pray. It annoyed him, knowing that they both shared the same underground home, but he felt more imprisoned than her. It was hard not to feel sorry for her though. Being stuck in a ten by ten cell, would have sent him insane, well before now.

A message flashed on his wristband. "Code 3."

"Damn it!" he said, rising to his feet.

"What's the matter?" Rex asked, looking up from his bench. "A bone in your potato?"

He laughed. "Emergency," Greg replied. "I can't even finish a meal in peace."

He leaned over and shovelled a spoonful of meat and potato into his mouth before leaving. When he arrived at the operations room, Scott was barking orders.

"What's happening?" Greg asked, entering the room.

"We have a situation at the front gate."

Greg looked at the monitors displaying live images of protesters climbing the outer boundary fence.

"Heck!" Greg looked around the room. "On foot, they could reach us in an hour."

"Our support team has shoot-to-kill orders, and I've also requested air support," Scott said.

"Scott, you can't be serious?" Greg looked at the others. "That's extreme measures for a group of unarmed protesters."

"Greg, this isn't a school camp. These hoodlums are intruding on a military base. We're authorized to defend ourselves in any way we find appropriate." He glared at Greg, "And I plan to do whatever it takes to protect these premises." He looked down at his phone. "Let me know when you hear back from the air support," he said, walking off to answer the call.

Elm Street, McLean, Virginia

"Scott, what's happening?" Cruse asked.

"You've called in the middle of a situation here," Scott said, agitated. "2000 activists have just breached the outside perimeter."

"God, damn it!" Cruse cursed, "I'm sitting in my favourite restaurant, about to enjoy a meal, with two national security advisors arriving any minute."

"Don't worry. We'll handle this."

"Just clean up any mess you make. I've got enough on my plate with Susan Banks," Cruse whispered, trying to keep his voice from being heard by those who were sitting nearby. "I'm warning you Scott, if this goes sour, I'm cutting you loose." He paused. "The Flashlight project will go ahead with or without you."

He ended the call, anxiously biting the side of his lip, and rising to his feet. "Cancel dinner," he said, as a young hostess approached. He reached for his jacket. "I've just had something urgent come up."

He was in the middle of putting his jacket on, when Susan walked in.

"Hello, Mr. Cruse," Susan said, folding her arms. "I believe we have met before."

Cruse looked around. "What is this?" He hated surprises.

"I'm as surprised by our meeting as you are, but I do have a small gift for you." Susan removed a small flash drive from her pocket.

"We can talk in my car," he said, wanting to take control of the environment.

Susan pulled a face to display her scepticism. "Would I really be willing to trust someone who was trying to arrest me less than 72 hours ago?"

Cruse shook his head in disbelief, taking a step forward to leave. "You have no evidence of anything you claim," he snapped.

"Really?" Susan said, holding up a small flash drive.

Cruse turned to face Susan front on, pointing in her face. "You're a risk to our national security."

"I hate to disappoint you Mr. Cruse, but the last time I was in America, I was in police protection. So, you'll have a lot of talking to explain how I've now become a threat to the nation." She looked at the flash drive. "Unless you're referring to the Flashlight list." She threw the flash drive towards him.

"We'll be seeing each other again, Miss Banks," he said, bending down to retrieve the flash drive. He turned to leave.

"Good night, Sir," the young hostess said.

Cruse ignored her and marched toward the door, clearly disturbed at how the evening had progressed. He stopped at the door, raising his finger in a threatening motion at Susan. As he stepped outside, the cold air slapped his face, and he was blinded by several floodlights.

"What the…"

Two men emerged from the darkness.

"Robert Cruse?"

"What's going on here?" Cruse asked, disoriented by the spotlights.

"This is Agent Randal James, from the internal investigation unit."

He held his badge toward Cruse. "You're being arrested on charges of treason."

The other man stepped forward with handcuffs.

"Please remove your firearm."

Cruse removed his gun and placed it in the agent's hand. As they led Cruse to their vehicle, the agents looked back at the building.

"Between subtle shading and the absence of light, lies the nuance of illusion," Randal said.

Cruse recognised the quote from the sculpture that sat in front of his office; 1000 Colonial Farm Road, Langley, Virginia, CIA headquarters.

CHAPTER 27

Delta Bunker, Nevada Desert

UNAWARE OF THE drama taking place above her, Kim sat motionless in the corner of her tiny cell. Observing her through a monitor screen, Greg might have previously been impressed by her remarkable inner strength and sense of peace, but right now he was concerned with her physical health.

The cell door opened and Greg stepped inside. He stared at Kim's body curled up body in the corner. She was oblivious to his presence. "Kim!"

As Greg knelt beside her, Kim woke from her inner world.

"Kim, I need you to listen to me."

She opened her eyes, trying to focus on Greg's face.

"Kim, can you hear me? If you can understand me, squeeze my hand."

She stared at Greg in a delirious state.

"Dehydration," Greg said.

He left Kim and hurried to the medical room. Several minutes later, he returned with an intravenous drip and stand. He inserted a needle into her arm and checked the bag of saline fluid. "Damn," he said, checking the time. It wouldn't be too long before he was missed on the upper floor. In the current state of emergency, everyone was focused on the protesters outside, but it wouldn't be long till they realised he had disabled the cameras on the lower level housing prisoners. Greg was deep in thought as he made his way back to the main hallway. He unlocked one of the cells. A young man with short black hair and glasses sat inside.

"Ricky."

The young man remained silent.

"Ricky, in the next hour this place is going to erupt."

"What do you mean?"

"Listen carefully. I'm going to try and help everyone escape, but I need your help."

"Why should I trust you?"

"If we sit around debating, we're both dead," Greg said, raising his voice to get Ricky's attention. He didn't wait for a reply. "I need you to open the other cells using this access card."

Ricky nodded.

"There should be 24 people."

"Okay, I can do that," Ricky said, as Greg handed him the card.

"Kim Knox, the lady with a drip in her arm, will need someone to help her."

Greg held out his pistol. "You know how to use a gun?"

"My father taught me," Ricky replied, still stunned by Greg's proposal.

"Great. When everyone is free, I need you to take them left down the hallway and wait for me inside the last room at the very end."

Ricky nodded.

"I'll be back to collect everyone from that room. Got it?"

Ricky looked at the pistol as Greg placed it in his hands.

"You'll be okay. Let's just hope you don't need to use that."

He slapped Ricky on the shoulder. "Okay, I'm going." He turned and ran down the hallway. "The last room at the very end!" he repeated.

****

Above the bunker, Lieutenant Randy Lambert was preparing his team of 30 commandos to engage the protestors. With the sky now dark, the only sound was desert insects.

"How's the weather boys?"

"All clear here, Boss. What are these protesters planning anyway? Are they going to club us to death with their signs?"

There was laughter in the background from several other men.

"Let's not get too relaxed. Stay alert."

"Any news from Drongo and Billy?"

"Nothing yet, but I'm sure the boys will keep us in the loop."

"Godfather, you picking up anything on infrared?"

"Our drones have the protestors located at seven kilometres away."

"Okay, keep me updated."

A short distance away, Thomas watched silently behind a small sand ridge, using night vision to see, and cloaking technology to avoid detection. "Let's see what these babies can do," he said, removing several small insect-like robots from a bag beside him.

"These things could steal the crown jewels," Zach, one of Thomas' team whispered.

The small machines were fitted with thermo sensors, and a special skin cover that changed its temperature to match the air and surrounding sand. Thomas held the controller and watched the tiny robots crawl over the ridge.

"Jericho is mobile," Zach said.

CHAPTER 28

THOMAS TAPPED A SMALL switch and stared at a small monitor, which moved with activity. He adjusted the display.

"And?" Zach whispered, busy adjusting another panel of knobs.

"Working perfectly," Thomas replied.

As the protesters approached the compound from the west, Thomas's silent army of insect robots, approached from the east. Extremely fast and manoeuvrable, the small machines navigated their way across the sand, communicating with each other using sounds undetectable to the human ear.

****

Greg made his way to the opposite end of the bunker which held the scientists. A green light shone, indicating that all prisoners were in their cells. Greg used his entry card to open the first cell door. The cell's occupant was startled by his unexpected visitor. The two men stared at each other as Greg entered.

"Fred, I'm here to help you escape," Greg said.

Fred Hallows was well known for his research in the field of Laser technology. Fred rose to his feet and followed Greg out of the cell.

"We have to hurry."

"Why are you doing this?" Fred asked.

"Kim Knox." Greg stopped to look Fred in the eyes. "I'm doing this for Kim Knox."

He quickly moved from one cell to the next. As the cell doors opened, the men stepped into the hallway looking at each other with confusion.

"Listen up people!" Greg looked around making sure he had their attention. "The bunker is under attack. I'm here to help you escape and send you home, but I need your help."

"Why are you doing this?"

Greg looked around at the faces. "I grew a conscience."

The men broke into lively conversation.

"There are only two exits to the building," Greg said, raising his voice to silence the men. "There's the main entrance which is well guarded, and an air shaft that runs through the middle of the building and leads to the surface."

"An escape is too risky," someone called out.

Greg took a step forward. "This place doesn't exist on paper, and if the public knew about it, it would be a nightmare for the government to explain. They would rather burn the place and believe me; these walls are fitted with enough explosives to sink the Titanic a hundred times over." He looked around the room. "I'm not suggesting this will be easy, but now is your best chance to try. Who's with me?"

An older man with a short grey beard and glasses raised his hand. "Can we all fit through the air shaft?"

"The shaft is almost a metre wide, so it shouldn't be a problem," Greg replied. He moved across to where Alfred was standing.

Alfred shook his hand in a display of trust. "What about security sensors inside the shaft?"

"Security can be overridden. I have the access codes."

Alfred looked at the others. "Greg is right. The main entrance will be crawling with security. The air shaft is our best chance."

"I can access rope," Greg said, "but we'll need someone willing to climb inside and secure the rope at the top." He waited for a volunteer and a young man stepped forward.

"I can climb."

"What's your name son?"

"Terry."

"Great. We also need something to cut through the mesh at the top."

"If we have access to the laboratory, we can find something."

"No problem," Greg said.

"We'll also need a diversion. Michael, is the Dragonfly VII prototype ready?" Alfred asked.

"There's a hundred ready for trial."

"Great. The trial starts today."

"There's one more thing," Greg said, pausing. "Scott has called an air strike with sarin gas. If I can't stop him, you'll need masks and protective suits. There are enough masks for everyone in the end storage room. Not sure about suits."

The room fell silent.

"Any questions?"

Alfred stepped forward. "Okay everyone, we have work to do. Let's move it."

Greg touched Alfred's shoulder. "I know where Kim is. Follow me."

They ran back through the corridors. Greg stopped at the supply room to access a large roll of rope. "Turn right. Kim should be in the first room. I'll leave the rope here!" Greg yelled. "I'm going to buy us some more time."

They exchanged glances before Greg ran toward the elevator.

"Good luck. And thanks!" Alfred called.

Alfred ran through the hallway in the direction that Greg had pointed. As he approached the room, he felt his heart pumping. He swung the door open and looked around at the room full of people.

"Kim!"

"Over here!" Ricky yelled.

Kim recognized Alfred's voice and looked up. Alfred dropped to the ground and embraced Kim in his arms.

"We're going home, Honey," he said, staring into her weary eyes.

They made their way back through the passageways, Ricky supporting Kim on one side, Alfred on the other. One of the other men collected the rope, and they headed toward the air shaft. The corridor outside was filled with people. They had to get more than 80 people up a shaft that was five stories high. He looked down the corridor shaking his head.

"There's too many of us." He looked at the bewildered faces. "And we still have no way to get through the mesh up top."

"You mean this isn't good enough?"

Two young men stepped forward carrying a large portable cutting laser. Everyone stepped back as they pointed their machine toward the wall. A loud cracking sound filled the air, as the machine effortlessly cut through the wall.

"Terry's up! He made it!"

"Where's Michael?" Alfred asked.

"He's with a few guys in the laboratory."

"Okay, we should expect visitors any minute. I'll go help the others." He bent down, kissing Kim's forehead.

Leonard, known for his work with radar technology and guidance systems, moved forward. "I'll come with you," he said, rubbing his bald head. A line of hair ran above his ears and around the back of his head.

"Me too," Marvin said.

Marvin worked with Alfred in the area of cloaking technology. The three men ran back through the corridors and approached Alfred's work station.

"We just need a way in," Alfred said.

"Stand back!"

The room shook as Marvin hit the glass door with a chair.

"It's bullet proof," Alfred said.

They stared at each other.

"Try this," Leonard said, stepping forward and swiping a card to open the door.

"How on earth?"

Leonard smiled, and Alfred led the small group to his workspace. He lifted a small box off one of the shelves.

"What on earth are they?" Andy asked, picking up one of the tiny robotic objects.

"Careful," Alfred warned. "I call them Nano Dragons."

"Holy cactus!"

"They're designed to pursue any moving object that produces heat, and sting it to death." He turned to see the reactions. "Okay, I need someone to place these around the elevator doors." He placed the small box into Andy's arms, without waiting for him to volunteer.

"I'm safe, aren't I?" Andy asked, looking petrified.

Alfred smiled. "Just be nice to them, Andy. Here's the control box." He placed a pair of silver overalls on top of the box with the controller.

"The suit will disguise your body's heat and you'll be safe when the Dragons are active. Wait until someone sticks their nose out of the elevator, and then hit this switch."

"Okay, got it," Andy said, staring at the controls.

CHAPTER 29

SCOTT WAS STARING at the monitors as Greg walked in. "Where have you been?" he said, catching the sight of Greg out of the corner of one eye.

Greg froze at Scott's stare, but they were interrupted.

"Sir, we just lost all our internal cameras."

Scott returned to the monitors. "Damn it!" he said, feeling frustrated.

"Randy on line one!" Drew called out.

Scott grabbed the phone. "Randy, it's Scott here. What's up?"

"We have a visual on the protesters."

"How many?"

"Initial estimate is 1600. There's more still…"

Scott interrupted. "We have an airstrike coming in 50 minutes. Stay put and have your gas masks ready."

"What are we talking?"

"GB."

"Sarin gas?"

Scott remained silent.

"You can't be serious," Randy said.

"Like I said, have your masks ready."

"Scott's a damn idiot!" Randy yelled, as he ended the call. "This night is going to end my career." He shook his head, frustrated by the position he found himself. He had sworn an oath to protect American citizens, not to kill them.

"What's the matter boss?" Godfather asked. "Scott shovelling sand in your mouth again."

"Not funny. If this goes sour, we are all going to wish we were back in Iraq," Randy said. As it was, he often wished he was back in Iraq. The Nevada Desert didn't offer as much entertainment.

****

"The main ventilation shaft is showing a breached entry," one of Scott's team observed. "But it could be just sand. We've had problems before."

"It's calm outside tonight. Shouldn't be sand," Drew replied.

"I'll go check," Greg said, turning to exit the operations room.

"Don't stop to brush your teeth this time."

Greg stopped at the door, calling over his shoulder, "I never even finished my meal." He walked to his office, closed the door and sat at his desk. For a brief moment he stared at the phone in front of him, finally lifting it to make a call. He tapped his fingers on the table top as he waited.

"Doug, it's Greg here."

"Greg, how's Nevada? I haven't heard from you in a while. What can I do for you?"

Greg and Doug had served in the air force together, previous to Greg's recruitment.

"I need a personal favour," Greg said. "We have around 1600 anti-war protesters marching toward us and Scott's ordered an airstrike with GB." He paused.

"Good grief!" Doug replied. "Sarin. Are you serious?"

"They're in the air now."

"Who has the power to authorize something like that?"

"CIA Deputy Director, Robert Cruse."

"What do you want me to do?" Doug whispered. "You realise we shouldn't even be having this conversation."

"Doug, we need to stop this."

"Oh man, Greg, do you realise what you're asking? I'm putting my neck on the line just talking to you." He sighed. "How much time do we have?"

"About 50 minutes," Greg said.

"Look, I'll make some inquiries and see what I can do," he whispered.

"Thanks Doug. Look I have to go, but there's one last thing. We run a black site with 80 prisoners. Their only crime is their IQ. I want to help them escape. If you don't hear…"

"Greg, that's suicide. I don't want to hear." He paused. "Take care, man."

Drew looked at Scott with a puzzled look. "Wasn't Greg supposed to be checking the air shaft? There's a secure call being made from his office."

"Where is he now?" Scott asked, moving toward the door.

"He just finished the call."

Greg and Scott met in the walkway outside the elevator.

"What in God's name are you doing?" Scott asked.

Greg stared at Scott. "I'm heading down to check the air shaft."

"And what have you been doing for the last five minutes?" Scott asked, his face turning red.

Greg remained silent.

"You made a secure call from your office, and I'm keen to know who, and why."

"You're about to kill 1600 American citizens, without any conscience," Greg replied.

"Sometimes you do things for the greater good," Scott said.

"You're a monster. You talk about the greater good, without having any moral compass."

The elevator stood opened and Greg looked inside.

"I'm sorry to hear that, Greg."

Scott closed the elevator door and touched his wrist communicator.

"Drew, I need you and one of the security guys at the elevator."

He stared into Greg's eyes, raising his firearm, and pointing it into Greg's face.

"This place is just a glorified prison," Greg said.

"You still haven't answered my question." Scott moved his pistol forward. "Who were you calling?"

Greg remained silent.

"So, you want to play hero. Well, we'll find out, and when we do, I'll be back to hang your scalp in the desert."

Drew arrived with a young security guard.

"Restrain him in one of the holding rooms, then go check the ventilation shaft."

Scott entered the room just as Marcus leapt to his feet. "We need people downstairs!"

"What's happening?"

"Cameras are still offline, both cell blocks are showing open, and someone has access to the lab," Marcus said, running toward the firearms cabinet.

"Damn! Lockdown people!" Scott shouted. "Greg's been playing the mole."

Michelle initiated the lockdown procedure, causing thick sliding walls to block the hallways on all the lower floors. As the hallways closed, Alfred and several colleagues were separated from the group.

Scott's team moved inside the elevator.

"Okay people, be ready, we don't know how many of these cells are empty."

Seconds later, they reached the lower level.

"Marcus, you and I will take the left, Drew and Gonzo, take the right."

Outside the elevator, Andy rested his finger on a small silver switch ready to activate the Nano Dragons which he had spread over the floor.

"On my count," Scott said. "Three, two, one!"

The doors of the elevator slid open and the air buzzed with the sound of small wings. Tiny needles protruding from the front of the flying machines, pierced the skin of their faces, neck, and arms. The elevator was filled with cursing as the men waved their arms in defence. As the Nano Dragons continued to inflict pain, Scott closed the elevator doors. Sounds of screaming travelled through the hallways as the elevator opened on control level. Other team members ran to help, but they were also attacked. Michelle and several others ran back inside the control room, locking the door, and swatting at two Dragons that had followed them inside. The main hallway leading to the control room, had now become a writhing mass of bodies, twisting on the floor to avoid the tiny machines. Inside the safety of the control room, Toni stood near a monitor observing the attack.

"We need to do something!"

Michelle held up one of the small Nano machines which had been crushed. "What are these things?"

Mark, another member of the team, held out his hand. "Nano Dragons," he said, studying the small object. "They pursue body heat and inject poison."

The few remaining people in the room stared in horror.

"It's fine, they won't die. We don't stock poison here," he said, turning to the monitor and watching the bodies of his colleagues screaming in pain. "They have about thirty minutes of electrical charge, so it won't be safe to leave this room for a while."

They watched the monitors with agonizing expressions, knowing that they could do nothing to help.

****

Outside the bunker, Randy called one of his men. "Drongo, what's the status report?"

"It looks like they're turning back."

Randy was puzzled. "Are you sure?"

"Positive. We have clear vision of all the protesters making their way back toward the main gate."

"Well, that's good news," Randy replied, "Follow them, and keep me updated. If anyone stops to do a pee, I want to know."

"Right boss."

Randy called the control room below, and Michelle put the call on loudspeaker.

"I have some good news. We have a visual of all the protesters returning to the main gate."

There were stares of disbelief around the control room.

"Randy, this is Michelle here."

"Michelle, we have an all clear on the ground," Randy said. "Cancel the airstrike."

"Randy, Scott and seven other colleagues are currently down. Alive but in pain."

"What happened?"

"Some miniature flying robots got loose.

"Hell! Do you need any back up?" he asked.

"We'll be fine for now, but just stay alert. I'll have Scott call you back."

CHAPTER 30

INSISDE THE LOWER level of the bunker, Alfred and three others were trapped between the sliding security walls. A flashing red light in the hallway was adding to his frustration.

Leonard pointed. "We could try the ceiling."

They lifted Leonard to examine the ceiling.

"What does it look like?" Alfred asked.

The bright ceiling lights caused Leonard to squint through his thick glasses. He knocked on the ceiling vent to gauge the thickness.

"It's doable, but we need a way to break through the covering," he said, as they lowered him back to the floor.

"We might find something in one of the rooms," Alfred said, hitting a button next to a door beside him. The door remained closed.

Michael joined Marvin and stood against the opposite wall. "Stand back guys," they said, launching themselves at the door with full force. The door shook, indicating that it was much thinner than the security barriers.

"Let's all try," Alfred said, encouraging an attempt by the whole group.

They hit the door again, this time creating a large split down the centre. They moved back for a third attempt. As they connected with the door, it broke and pushed forward.

They pushed the pieces of the door aside and entered the room.

"The bookshelf!"

They all turned.

"It's worth a try," Alfred said.

They leaned the shelf forward, allowing the contents to crash on the floor, and re-entered the hall. As they thrust the bookshelf into the ceiling, the air vent cover buckled upward.

"Leonard, you first," Alfred said.

They helped each other up and into the ceiling.

****

Above ground, Randy received a call from Scott, and sent two of his men to check the air shaft entrance.

"Boss, you better come," one of the men said, as they approached the small building covering the shaft. "We have movement inside."

Randy took another man with him.

"If anyone managed climbing the ventilation shaft, they would have a nasty surprise waiting. The fan at the top spins fast."

They moved in closer towards the small building that covered the shaft.

"I can't hear the fan," one of them whispered.

Suddenly, a loud sound ripped through the air as a cutting laser burned through the outer wall. Everyone in the compound dropped to the ground.

"Holy cow!" one of men shouted.

"What was that!"

Randy raised his rifle. As his men slowly approached the small building, there was complete silence inside.

"We have the building surrounded!" Randy yelled. "You're inside a military compound, and we have orders to shoot and kill."

He signalled one of the men to approach the large steel access door.

"Lay down your weapons and no one gets hurt!" he called out. "Can anybody hear me?"

"Yes!"

"I need everyone inside to call out their names," he said, hoping to get an idea of numbers.

Tension filled the air as each soldier focused the red dot of their laser sights on the side of the building. There was a moment of silence before those inside responded.

"James Warwick."

"Matthew Green."

"Kurt Benson."

"Terry Matheson."

There was a pause of silence.

"Is that all?" Randy asked.

"Just four of us."

"Okay, and who am I talking to?"

"James."

"Okay James, this is Lieutenant Randy Lambert. We don't' want anyone getting hurt, so I need you guys to do a few things to help us out." He paused. "Are you hearing me?"

"We hear you."

"Okay, James, that's great. First, we need you to drop weapons or anything else you might be holding." He waited for a response.

"We're ready."

"That's great, James." Randy motioned his men closer. "In a moment we will open the door, and I'll need everyone to place their hands on their heads. When you've done that, let me know." One of the soldiers stood at the door awaiting orders. Randy gave the signal and the door was unlocked. "Okay, James. What's happening? Talk to me."

"Our hands are on our heads."

Randy and the other soldiers positioned themselves around the door and he signalled the door to be opened.

"Okay James, I need everyone walking slowly from the building, one by one, and lying face down. Are you with me?"

James was the first to exit the building and lay on the ground. The three other men followed and two of Randy's men checked inside.

"All clear!"

They handcuffed the four men and led them into one of the compound buildings.

"Listen up everyone. Stay alert. I have a feeling this night isn't over yet," Randy said.

****

Inside the bunker, Michelle and the other staff were assisting their wounded colleagues. Scott wiped drops of blood from his face and hands. "Have we got those cameras working yet?" he asked.

"We have two guys working on it," Michelle replied, observing Scott's misery with horror on her face. "Randy just apprehended four men trying to escape through the main ventilation shaft, but it's now secure."

"Great," Scott replied, rolling his eyes upward. Still feeling dazed, he took another tissue and wiped the blood between his fingers. "Damn Nano Dragons!"

****

Alfred made his way through the ceiling. "Straight ahead and to the right," he said to Michael, who was leading the way.

The men reached an intersection.

"It's hard on your knees."

"Yer, I feel like a worm wriggling around in here," Michael complained.

"So, you mean that three years underground didn't already give you that feeling?" Alfred replied.

"Ten points for that observation."

Alfred rubbed his knee. "If I'm correct, we should be very close to the others."

They continued to move through the ceiling, stopping to peer through each air vent.

****

"How long have you been here?" Ricky asked Kim.

The colour had now returned to Kim's face and she was sitting up. "It's hard to keep track of time, but I've had thirteen meals," she replied. She looked at Ricky's dark brown eyes. "And you?"

"If my calculations are correct, 728 days," Ricky said, looking at the floor.

Kim reached over and touched his arm in a gesture of mutual support. "Don't give up hope," she said. "Because hope is all we have."

He looked around at the others. "Do you think we'll ever be free from this place?"

Kim smiled. "It's hard to see anything positive by only focusing on problems." She paused. "I try to celebrate every day, because it means I'm still alive. And while I'm alive, there is hope." She pulled the saline stand closer. "Every day I remain undefeated means I am stronger than my enemy." She took a deep breath. "And while I wait to be rescued. God is working within me and giving me inner strength." She squeezed Ricky's arm. "At least that's what I tell myself on the good days."

"In the winter of life, we find an indelible summer within," Ricky added.

"Exactly!"

"A quote I learned from my father."

"Your father sounds very wise," Kim said.

"He is. My mother died when I was really young, so father raised my sister and I. I learned so much from him."

"I'm sorry to hear about your mother," Kim replied. "Your father sounds like a wonderful man."

"He spent lots of time with us, and took us all around the world. Spain, Italy, Greece, England, America, even China."

"I pray that God reunites us with our families," Kim said, thinking of her sister Lynne and her two boys.

Suddenly, they heard a voice in the air duct above them.

"Hey! Is anyone going to help us down?"

"It's Alfred!"

Several men jumped to their feet.

"Move back guys! We're going to get you out."

They struck the air vent cover, and after several attempts, bent the cover downwards. Slowly, they lowered Alfred and the other men to the floor.

Alfred ran to Kim. "What's happening?"

"Security stopped our escape."

Alfred's face showed disappointment.

"But we're together," she said, squeezing him tight.

CHAPTER 31

S COTT RETURNED TO the operations room. "Give me Randy," he said, dabbing antiseptic pads on his face to ease the pain. He looked around the room. "How are the others?" he asked.

"Everyone came out okay, except for Drew."

"What happened?"

"His left eye was hit bad."

Scott shook his head. "Are those cameras back online yet?"

"Another minute," one of the team shouted, from a wiring panel.

"Several cables were cut," Michelle added.

Randy answered Scott's call. "How are things down below?"

"Licking our wounds, but we'll be fine. What's the status up top?"

"All clear here, but we're not sleeping tonight."

"Keep us informed of any new developments." As he ended the call, his private phone rang. "Hello?"

"Scott, I have bad news." It was Berkley. "Cruse was arrested an hour ago on charges of treason." There was silence. "Scott, you need to lay low for a while. Are you hearing me?"

"I hear you, Sir," Scott replied, rolling his head backward and rubbing his neck.

"Flashlight is over, Scott. Follow backup procedures and close up shop." Scott's face turned pale. He dropped the phone, and suddenly the monitors in front of him came alive.

"We're back online," Michelle announced, looking at the monitors.

"Where is everyone?"

Michelle switched between camera feeds.

"They can't have just disappeared," Scott said.

The whole room was now staring at the main display screen.

"Someone talk to me. Why are we looking at empty corridors?"

Everyone stared at each other.

"There's 187 cameras down there," Toni said.

"243," Michelle corrected. "We placed cameras under all workbenches and inside the cupboards two months ago."

"Over there," Scott said, "Zoom in."

The camera zoomed closer.

"Who's that?"

"Andrew Marring," Michelle replied. "Looks like he was separated from the others."

"Michelle, run a systems backup and initiate evacuation procedures. Toni, request Creech Air Base to dispatch three Blackhawk's." All eyes were on Scott. "Cruse has been arrested. Flashlight's dead. If the rest of those misfits are hiding down there, this place is about to become their tomb."

"Self-destruct?" Michelle asked, trying to clarify.

"Yes. Berkley's orders."

"What about Greg?"

"Greg knows too much. We can't afford deserters. This place will be a convenient graveyard for him too."

Scott left the room and met Greg in the room where he was being restrained.

"Greg," he paused. "Have you got any last words to say?"

Greg stared at Scott. "So, this is it. I never expected my government career to end with a bullet in the head."

Scott laughed. "I'm not here with any bullets. Although when I close this door, you might wish I had put a bullet through your skull." He placed his hands on his hips and grinned. "In the last few minutes of your pitiful life, I want you to agonize over the consequences of betrayal."

"I will die with an innocent conscience," Greg said, staring into Scott's eyes. "You're not serving your country. You're serving greed, ego and the lust for power."

Scott sneered at him, then turned and left the room, leaving Greg handcuffed and tied to a chair.

****

Thomas observed Randy and his men loading equipment onto the back of several trucks.

"It looks like they're evacuating," Thomas said, adjusting his cameras for a better view. "This could end really bad."

"What's the plan?" Zach asked.

"We sit tight," he replied. "We're not leaving until we complete our mission."

Several minutes later, Scott and his team appeared at the main bunker entrance. Thomas watched the trucks moving through the large gates and out of the compound. At the same time three helicopters appeared, landing beside the road a short distance from the trucks. Scott's team abandoned the trucks, and entered the helicopters. The trucks drove into the distance, and within minutes the area returned to silence.

"Okay, let's move it guys!" Thomas shouted. "Those choppers can only mean one thing. This place is likely to explode any minute."

The men ran toward the front gate which had been left opened. Inside the compound, they headed directly toward the building where Thomas had seen the four men escorted.

"Over here!" one of the guys yelled.

The four men were tied and lying on the floor.

"Okay guys, let's move it!"

Two of Thomas' team cut the men free and helped them to their feet.

"I hope you men can run, cause you'll have a burnt backside if you're too slow."

The group of men ran at full speed toward the main gate and down the road. In their haste, one of the men dropped his glasses, and stopped.

"Come on, Pops! Let's move it!" Zach shouted.

One hundred metres down the road, they reached a small ridge.

"Take cover guys!" Thomas ordered.

There was a mad scramble and the men dropped to the ground. As they struggled to regain their breath, Thomas peered over the top of the ridge.

"I almost killed myself running," one of the men complained, still panting heavily.

Thomas pressed a button on his small communicator, "Kameel, it's Thomas here. What's happening your end?"

"The puppet show is over," Kameel replied.

Suddenly, a loud explosion shook the ground, and a ball of intense fire blasted upward, lighting the desert with a golden glow. A rush of hot air hit the men, and a layer of sand showered their bodies. They lay with arms over their heads, not daring to move until the sand shower stopped. Then one by one, they rose to their feet, brushing themselves. Fragments of burning rubble were scattered all around them.

"Are you guys still alive?" Kameel asked.

"We're covered in an inch of sand, but we're alive," Thomas said, shining his headlamp toward the others.

"What just happened?"

"The puppet theatre just closed for the night," Thomas replied, wiping his forehead.

"May our fallen companions rest in peace," one of the rescued men said.

"Your friends are all safe. Probably enjoying a drink and waiting for us."

The four men looked at each other.

"What do you mean?" James asked.

"We're going to see your friends now," Thomas replied.

"I don't understand."

Thomas grabbed him by the shoulders. "You're a free man."

The four scientists looked at each other with stunned expressions.

"You're all free men!" Thomas yelled, above the noise of the fire.

They burst into laughter, and embraced each other in celebration.

CHAPTER 32

Langley, Virginia

AS SUSAN ENTERED her hotel room, her thoughts were interrupted by the phone ringing. Only one person had her number.

"Graham?"

"Susan, I know it's late. Have you heard the latest from Nevada?"

"No. What's happening?"

"Switch on the television," Graham said, his words racing.

"Graham, I've just been questioned for the last three hours. Cruse has been arrested," she said calmly.

There was silence as Graham collected his thoughts.

"Cruse was arrested?"

"Yes. A few hours ago."

"On what charges?"

"Treason. The whole thing is about to be exposed. I have a recording of Cruse talking with Scott Denman, the project director at Delta Bunker."

"There may not be a bunker anymore," Graham replied. "Apparently, the activists broke through the perimeter fence, and there's reports of a large explosion."

Susan's hand shook. "I wasn't aware."

"Look, no one can really say for sure. Military training areas are off limits for journalists, so it may take a little time before we really know what happened."

"Keep me updated, if you can."

"Yes, likewise," Graham replied, detecting sadness in Susan's voice. He ended the call, leaving Susan alone in her thoughts.

Susan stood on the balcony looking down at the colourful lights shining through the cover of the outdoor pool. It was close to midnight and she realised she had not eaten, but the thought of food didn't excite her tonight. She stared at the city skyline one last time before returning inside and hitting the TV remote. The television came alive with images of protesters in Nevada, and what appeared to be fire in the distance. She switched the television off and stared at the blank screen.

It was the end of a long journey. A journey that had up to this point, offered few rewards, yet continually demanded all that she had. She clenched her fists in anger and tossed a cushion across the room. Releasing a flood of tears, she remembered Raheem's words. 'Respond from the motive of moral duty, not revenge'. They were words that she had lived by during the last few months, yet now it appeared that moral duty had failed. With the help of some clever lawyers, Cruse would probably escape all charges and walk away free. Meanwhile, she had lost everyone she loved. She collapsed on the bed. "Why God?" she asked.

****

"Scott, it's Eric. The intelligence team just intercepted a call between Susan Banks and the journalist in New York."

"Susan Banks?"

"Yes. He spoke to her about Nevada. We traced the receivers call to a hotel here in Langley."

"Langley! That woman has some guts," Scott replied.

"One more thing, Banks was involved in Cruse's arrest.

"I'm on my way to Langley now. You've got guys at the hotel?"

"They arrived ten minutes ago."

"Stay with her, but don't do anything before I get there. And have a car waiting at the airport."

"Done, Sir," Eric said.

****

After breakfast the next day, Susan entered the elevator and a man stepped in behind her. Susan smelled his aftershave. It smelled strangely familiar. She dropped her pen on the floor, bumping it with her shoe and causing it to roll toward the back of the elevator. Susan glanced at the man, with a look that suggested he should offer to retrieve it. As the man bent down, Susan hit the emergency stop. The elevator door reopened and Susan ran, briefly looking over her shoulder. At the same time, a beeper in her handbag sounded its alarm, indicating that the motion sensor in her room had been triggered.

She ran toward the kitchen, with the man pursuing close behind, and burst through the doors. Several women screamed. At the far end of the kitchen, she entered a walk-in pantry and closed the door. Susan shook as the man entered. The kitchen staff stood paralysed. As the man opened the pantry, a loud gunshot exploded, causing the staff to scream and take cover behind a bench. Susan stepped from the pantry holding her small handgun and looked around the room in a state of shock. Her heart thumped madly.

"Please don't shoot," one of the staff said, shaking nervously. For a brief second their eyes connected, then Susan ran toward the exit door.

As she stepped outside, a silhouetted figure held a gun toward her. "Freeze!"

Driven by adrenaline, Susan returned inside, pushed her way through a large door, and ran up a flight of stairs that led to the first floor. She clung to her handbag and raced along the corridor, stopping at a room that was opened for cleaning. Inside the room, Susan took several deep breaths, then returned to the corridor and grabbed a bottle of cleaning liquid under the cleaners' trolley. As she did, two men appeared at the opposite end of the hallway. Susan ran back inside the room, locking the door behind her and heading to the balcony. She looked into the pool below and realised her room was on the level above. There was a loud bang on the door.

"Open up!"

She returned inside, emptying the contents of her handbag on the bed and taking the cash. A second later, the door was kicked open and the two men slowly entered.

"Miss Banks. We know you're in here."

One of the men approached the bed where Susan's bag lay. As he turned, Susan stepped from the bathroom and threw a glass of cleaning liquid into his face. The man fell to the ground, holding his eyes and screaming. The second man grabbed Susan's arm, twisting it, and forcing her to the ground. With her free hand, Susan reached inside her jacket, rolling her body at the same time. Her gun fired, and the man dropped to the ground holding his stomach. Susan pointed her gun at his face, and walked slowly backward toward the balcony. A second later, two more men appeared in the doorway with their guns drawn.

"Drop the gun!"

Susan obeyed, dropping the gun at her feet.

One of the men approached her, glancing down at his injured teammates as he passed by.

The second man called for help. "We have Banks. Two men down. Request medical assistance on level two."

"Okay lady, on the floor," the man insisted, carefully edging forward.

Susan clung to the rail of the balcony behind her and turned her head to look over the edge.

"Don't try anything stupid," he said.

"You people are mindless robots. You're trained to blindly follow orders without any conscience."

Susan swung her legs over the balcony.

"Stay where you are!"

He took a step forward.

"What are you going to do? Shoot me? Can't you see I'm unarmed?" Susan released the balcony rail and held both hands in the air.

The man took another step.

Susan smiled, then leapt outward. Her body dropped out of sight, then hit the pool cover below and bounced. The man hurried to the rail in time to see Susan crawling to the side of the pool.

"Damn!" He spun around and ran from the room. Two other men entered the hallway from the elevator. "She's out front!" he yelled, startling the cleaning woman who was peering from the opposite room to investigate the noise.

Susan jumped the pool fence and waved down a passing taxi. "Downtown," she said, dusting a lump of snow off her pants and jumping in.

The taxi driver stared at his rear-view mirror. "You look like you've been enjoying the snow."

She smiled and took a deep breath. "I've just finished my morning workout."

"Good for you. So, where are we headed?" the driver asked.

"Destiny," Susan replied.

"A dress shop?" he asked.

"Near Syracuse."

"To the airport then?"

Susan leaned forward handing him $1000 in one-hundred-dollar notes.

"My daughter is giving birth, but I'm afraid of flying."

The driver whistled, impressed by the sight of so much money.

"I'm not sure I can get you there before the birth," he replied.

"That's fine," she said, "I need time to work out what gift I should buy."

The taxi driver went along with the game. "Lady, I'm not really sure I believe your story, but if you pay for the fuel as well, we have a deal." He looked to the rear-view mirror.

"Done," Susan said. "Tell your boss you're busy with a sightseeing trip."

The driver laughed. "Yeah. Sightseeing trip." He shook his head in disbelief and glanced at the mirror again.

Eric was there to meet Scott at the airport.

"We lost her."

"Damn it! I told you guys to wait until I arrived. What happened?" A cloud of condensation filled the air as he spoke.

"Our guys had her bailed up in a room on the second floor. She jumped from the balcony and disappeared."

He shook his head. "Unbelievable. This woman has guts. I'll give her that," Scott said, as they walked briskly to an awaiting vehicle. Eric remained quiet. From his many years working with Cruse, he had learned that the less he said, the better.

"So, what's the latest?"

"She booked tickets to New York this morning, but failed to show up at the airport," Eric replied.

"Well, that's no surprise," Scott said, sarcastically.

"We're monitoring all transport out of the city, and Graham Harnold the New York Times reporter, is still under surveillance," Eric said.

"She's heading back to New York," Scott said, thinking aloud.

"Cruse's arrest is a big blow for everyone," Eric finally said.

"With Cruse gone, the game has changed," Scott replied.

"A lot of people are starting to get nervous," Eric said, looking across at Scott to observe his reaction.

"When the big fish are caught, the small fish panic. When the small fish panic." He glared at Eric, as a warning. "Just keep your pants zipped. One mistake and we'll all have our heads in the frypan."

****

Several hours later, Susan's driver stopped for a break.

"I have a request."

"What is it now?" the driver asked, holding a cup of coffee.

"I lost my credit card, and I would love to send a gift to my sister. It's her birthday. If I give you fifty dollars, could I use your card for an internet order?"

The taxi driver shook his head. "You're a bit of a mystery woman," he said, looking at her suspiciously.

"Look, I'm not out to scam you. I can pay my bills," she said, holding up a roll of notes. "There's an internet terminal inside. It'll only take two minutes."

"So, you want to send your sister a gift. Is that it?"

"Yes," Susan replied, hoping the driver would agree.

"I thought you said your sister was having a baby."

Susan's eyes pleaded with him. "This is really important."

"Fine, but this is a one-off exception," he said. "What would my wife say if she knew I was travelling the country with another woman, helping her buy gifts for family?" He laughed at the ridiculous situation he had got himself into.

****

In New York, Graham arrived at Starbucks, waited half an hour for Susan and left again. He was walking through the door of his office when one of his colleagues called.

"Graham!"

He turned to look.

"Delivery for you."

He took the package and continued walking to his desk. "Who on earth is Hannah Gessart?" he asked, looking at the senders' address.

One of the nearby desk clerks overheard. "Another secret admirer, Graham?"

Several laughs were heard around the office.

"Well, don't keep us in suspense," one of the ladies begged, pausing her data entry.

Graham opened the package with curious onlookers gathering around his desk.

CHAPTER 33

New York City

OUTSIDE THE NEW YORK TIMES head office, Drew and Marcus, were watching for any sign of Susan.

"Your face looks like a red balloon," Marcus said.

"Thanks for the reminder," Drew replied, unenthused by the fact that he looked like a side-show freak. He touched his eye patch. "I'll be having nightmares about those flying beasts for the next year."

"Our journalist friend has been back for about twenty minutes," Marcus observed. He reached down for his phone. "Jared, what's happening?"

"Nothing much in the paper," Jared replied.

Jared and two other men were positioned on the 14th floor of the Proskauer building, opposite the New York Times. Using a laser microphone and noise filtering technology, they were able to listen to individual conversations inside Graham's office.

"It's a good day at the office today," he said, referring to the signal strength. "Fred returned," he said, referring to Graham. "Received a package, got his fourth coffee for the day, and is now chatting about tomorrow's weather."

"Keep your eye on the weather," Marcus replied, "I have a feeling we're in for a change."

****

"Wake up, Cinderella. Your carriage has arrived."

Susan yawned. The city lights helped her brain ignite. "How long did I sleep?"

"The last two hours," the driver replied. "Becoming a grandmother would make me tired too." He chuckled, and adjusted his mirror for a better view of Susan.

She returned a smiled.

"Where do you want to be dropped off?"

"There's a nice hotel downtown. You can drop me there."

"Has it got a name?"

Susan looked out the window, mesmerized by the lights.

"The hotel?" he repeated.

"Destiny Palace," she said, continuing to stare out the window.

He entered the hotel name into his navigator. "You're a mystery, Lady," he said, looking at his mirror.

****

Graham was still trying to figure out the significance of the tiny toys on his desk.

"Why would anyone post me a set of Coyote and Road Runner figurines?"

One of his work colleagues stood. "Oh, oh, this is good," he said, dramatizing. "Graham has this secret lover who owns a toy store."

Laughter broke out around the office, and Graham threw one of the tiny figurines at him.

"Shut up, Bruce," another colleague responded. "Any parent can tell those toys only mean one thing."

The others joined him as if repeating a rehearsed chorus. "Graham is a daddy!"

Graham threw another two figurines at those sitting closest. After a few minutes, the office banter ended and everyone returned to their work. Graham stared at the one remaining toy Road Runner on his desk. Could Susan's non-appearance be related in some way? Susan had always been as reliable as the Times Square clock. Graham picked up the paper wrapping, and suddenly realised he had overlooked a tiny message inside.

"Choice not Chance, Determines Destiny."

He stared at the note, then jumped to his feet and grabbed his jacket.

"Hey, Graham. Where are you going?"

"The toy store," he said, sarcastically.

The office filled with laughter as he left the room.

CIA Headquarters, Langley, Virginia

Back in Langley, Scott was in the middle of yet another intense interview. He wasn't used to being on the opposite end of the interrogation table.

"We understand that your purpose at Delta Bunker was classified."

The interviewer glanced at Scott as he flicked through his notes.

"I've answered these questions before," Scott said, tapping his fingers on the desk.

"We still don't have a satisfactory reason why you would destroy a US government facility when it appears from all other reports, the protesters had retreated to the perimeter fence."

Scott looked at the interviewer emotionless. "I have no further comments to make. I've already stated that I was following strict protocol, under the direct orders of Robert Cruse, and I'm not required to disclose details in this setting."

"Cruse was in custody, Scott."

Scott was silent.

"Okay, let's wrap this up. We're not getting anywhere," the interviewer said, closing his file and preparing to leave.

He turned at the door.

"Don't leave Langley without my direct permission. Is that clear?"

Scott had a smug look on his face, knowing that no one had any right to restrict his travel without a proper legal directive. He walked from the interview room, relieved that it was finally over. Three hours of interviews had made him edgy.

Destiny USA, Syracuse, New York

"I'd offer to carry your bags, but you're a little light on the luggage," the driver said, parking outside the hotel.

He stopped the car to stretch his legs.

"I almost forgot." He reached into the taxi to retrieve a small bag. "I bought this at the last stop," he said, shyly. "For the baby."

Susan reached into the bag and pulled out a small stuffed penguin.

"Thank you," she said, hugging him in an awkward embrace.

A short time later, Susan stood in front of room 305, tapped the access card, and opened the door. She smiled as she considered checking into a hotel with a stuffed penguin and no luggage. She looked around, then opened the curtains to view the city lights. Her mind was flooded with images of the last time she had been in the same room. She stared at the large gold mirror, on which Tom had written a love note, and placed the small penguin on one of the pillows. Tom had arranged for the floor to be decorated with flower petals. Suddenly, the phone in her room rang.

"Susan, it's Graham. I'm down in the lobby."

"Graham? I'll be right there."

As she stepped from the elevator, Graham jumped from his seat.

"Graham, what are you doing here?"

"What do you mean?"

Susan looked around the lobby. "How did you find me?"

Graham's face morphed into a question mark. "You sent a message," he said.

Susan grabbed his arm and hurried toward the elevator. "Were you followed?"

The doors of the elevator conveniently opened and an elderly couple walked out.

"I'm not as paranoid as you, if that's what you mean," Graham said, shifting the shoulder strap of his laptop and stepping into the elevator.

"I never sent you any message."

He stared at her. "The plastic figurines. I received a parcel with a toy road runner and a message."

"I never sent a parcel."

"This is where you and Tom spent your honeymoon," Graham said. "The message was a quote about Destiny, so I figured that since you hadn't turned up for our meeting, you were telling me to come here."

The elevator opened and they stepped into the hallway.

"The only thing I sent today was flowers. Today is my cousins' birthday… and Tom. It's our anniversary."

"So, who sent the gift?" Graham asked.

"Perhaps someone that wanted us together."

"Hey, no, no, I'm not like that," Graham said, following Susan into the room.

Susan laughed. "Not romantically. Someone wants the information about Flashlight to go public," she said, peering through the curtains.

Graham paced nervously around the room. "So, what happened with Cruse?"

"I'm not sure who organized it all, but someone built a replica of Cruse's favourite restaurant and invited us both on a blind date." She laughed. "They had the room filled with actors."

They stared at each other.

"Did you find out anything?" Susan asked.

"My contacts said that Cruse was involved in some secret deals with Middle Eastern rebel groups, but there's still something missing. I get the feeling this is just the tip of the iceberg."

Their conversation was interrupted by a knock at the door. Susan looked at Graham.

"You're sure you weren't followed?" Susan asked, walking across the room to look through the curtains a second time.

Graham pushed his laptop under the bed, and a second later, the door opened with a loud crash. Two men in swat uniform entered with their guns drawn. They forced Susan and Graham into one corner and checked the bathroom and wardrobe.

"All clear!" one of them yelled.

Susan and Graham held each other.

"Susan Banks, what a surprise!" Scott said, as he marched into the room. "You've kept us busy chasing you around the world; and here you are, right in our own backyard." He shook his head. "Who would have guessed?"

The two armed men handcuffed Graham and moved toward Susan.

CHAPTER 34

I'VE HAD A NASTY week, but now that I have you in the basket, I can start to relax again," Scott said, looking at Susan as her hands were cuffed together. He turned to address Drew, as he walked through the door. "Notify the extraction team. Two packages ready for transport."

"Yes, Sir," Drew replied, relaying the message on his radio.

Scott moved toward Susan, grasping her chin in his hand, and meeting her eyes with a menacing stare. "A lot of old history is now buried, and you're the next."

Susan spat in Scott's face, causing him to step backward. He regained his composure, and slapped Susan's cheek.

"The men and women on the Flashlight list will never be forgotten," Susan said, glaring at Scott, with a small trail of blood now running from her lip.

"Flashlight is dead, and everyone connected to it," Scott replied, wiping his face. "Tell me the transport team are ready."

Scott signalled Drew to move along the hallway in front of him. As they approached the elevator, armed men suddenly appeared from nearby rooms and ambushed the group. Scott grabbed Susan and positioned himself against the wall with his arm around her neck, and a gun to her head. The two groups yelled at each other in a tense standoff.

"It's over Scott! Drop the weapons and let her go!"

Susan turned her head to see Thomas.

Scott looked behind. His team of five were outgunned. Three men blocked the path in front, and three behind.

"In case you haven't noticed, I have a gun pointed at your sweet lover's head." He tightened his grip around Susan's neck with his left arm. Susan squeezed her eyes close.

"You might want to check the serial number on that gun," Thomas replied.

Scott looked at Thomas with scepticism.

"I'm holding a pistol here, and if I'm not mistaken, the serial number is listed against your name."

Thomas held the gun in the air as Scott looked around to consider his options. He squeezed Susan's neck tighter, causing her to gasp for air.

Thomas checked the time, and nodded at Zach. Zach produced a small iPad.

"I thought you might all like to see a quick news update," Thomas said.

Zach tapped the screen, connecting to a live TV broadcast.

"You should recognise the venue," Thomas said, addressing Scott. "I believe it was the last place we met."

Scott stared at the small screen, pulling Susan closer and waiting for Thomas to make a slipup. A reporter stood in front of the nightclub in which Susan's look-a-likes had gathered six months before.

"Turn up the volume," Thomas said.

"If you've just joined us, we are broadcasting live from Lower Manhattan, where right now a press conference is about to take place," the reporter announced. "We understand there are about 80 scientists from around the world, all claiming they were abducted and kept in a secret military facility under the Nevada desert."

The camera panned to show the crowds of media.

"The White House is denying the claims, but we can expect this is only the beginning of many new revelations regarding similar operations funded by the US government."

Thomas lowered the volume as the broadcast continued.

"Impossible," Scott said.

"Is it also impossible to dig a thirty-kilometre tunnel under the desert?" Thomas asked. "It took us two hours transporting everyone out, but they all arrived safe, including Kim and Alfred Knox."

Susan stared wide eyed at Thomas.

"Kim and Alfred are alive and well," Thomas said.

Thomas addressed Scott's men.

"Drop the weapons and you might get suspended sentences for following orders." He waited patiently. "Come on guys, who are you loyal to? Your country, or Scott?"

Two of Scott's men dropped their weapons.

"Stay back Thomas!" Scott yelled, attempting to gain control of the situation. "You want your girl here alive. I'm warning you, step aside."

He squeezed Susan's throat causing her to gag. Drew and one other man held their weapons firm, anticipating a command.

"Say the word, Tommy," Kameel said, his gun aimed at one of Scott's men.

Thomas held up his hand.

"Okay, Scott. Have it your way," Thomas said. "Hand over the girl and we let you go."

Thomas stepped aside making a path for Scott to exit. Scott moved along the wall and inched his way past Thomas. Thomas's gun kept its mark on Scott's forehead. "Okay, Scott. Let her go."

Scott continued moving backwards down the hallway.

"Your gun is empty, Scott!" Thomas said, slowly following him. "Let her go."

"Stay there, Thomas! You know I can snap this woman's neck with one hand."

Susan opened her eyes, looking at Thomas. Not a word was communicated, but she took courage. As Scott pulled her backward, Susan moved her right leg around behind him, bent forward, and fell backwards causing Scott to trip. Thomas made a flying leap towards them, allowing Susan to roll free as he wrestled with Scott. Scott threw Thomas against the wall, reaching for his gun a short distance away. Susan screamed, and moved forward to kick the gun from his hand. The brief distraction enabled Thomas to position himself above Scott, pinning him to the floor. Scott struggled furiously, and managed to free himself, rolling away from Thomas and onto his feet.

As they eyeballed one another, Scott reached behind his back and produced a small knife from his belt.

"This ends tonight," Scott said, lunging at Thomas.

Susan manoeuvred her handcuffed arms in front and reached for a gun lying nearby. Thomas stepped back as Scott swung the knife blade. A moment later, another two men from Scott's team entered the hallway with their guns drawn. As Thomas turned to look, Scott caught him off guard, kicking one of Thomas's legs, and holding him to the floor.

"Victory always comes to the better man, Thomas." Scott said, holding his knife against Thomas' neck.

He glanced up at his two men, who had now equalled the balance of power. Suddenly, a shower of bullets thundered through the hallway, filling the air with smoke. Several bodies dropped to the floor. When silence returned, Thomas rose and looked around. Scott's lifeless body lay in a pool of blood beside him. Susan sat shaking on the floor, both hands grasping a small pistol in front of her.

Zach ran to check the bodies. "Kameel's down!"

Kameel lifted his head and smiled at Thomas. "It's just a scratch," he croaked.

Thomas sat next to Susan, removing the gun from her hands. "How did you know that was the right gun?"

"A lucky guess," Susan said, shaking.

Thomas placed an arm around her. "It's all over."

CHAPTER 35

Two months later

IT WAS A CLEAR blue sky as the occupants of the Sikorsky S-76C_helicopter lifted into the air.

"I'll take you past the Florida Keys," the pilot announced through his headset.

Susan held her Smartphone against the window, taking photos. The flight took them along the miles of beautiful shoreline, finally leaving any sight of land and heading out to sea.

Twenty-five minutes later, a cruise ship appeared in view.

"All clear for final approach and landing," a voice announced.

The pilot brought the helicopter over the landing area on one of the upper decks, and made his descent.

"That was an unforgettable experience!" Susan said, leaning toward Thomas to be heard.

"Glad you enjoyed it!" he replied, as they stepped onto the deck.

From one end of the ship a small group of people moved toward them.

"Kim!"

Susan ran to Kim and held her in a tight embrace.

"Great to see you again, Susan," Alfred said, joining the ladies in a welcoming hug.

Susan wiped the tears from her eyes.

"We have lots of catching up to do. How are things in New York?" Kim asked.

"I returned to the law firm a few weeks ago," Susan said, "And I'm also working for a charity."

"Interesting. You'll have to tell me more later."

"Come on ladies, let's go inside," Thomas said, inviting them all to follow him. "Unless you would like to enjoy the sun."

"Yes, please!" They said in unity.

Everyone laughed.

"After living underground, you appreciate sunlight," Alfred said.

He cupped his hands around his mouth. "Glorious sunshine!"

Kim kissed him on the cheek.

"Sunshine it is," Thomas said.

At that moment, two boys ran up to them.

"Dad! There's a games room downstairs!" the boy with sandy coloured hair said, grabbing his father around the waist in a show of affection.

A tear formed in Susan's eyes.

"Boys, say hello to Aunt Susan," Kim said.

Samuel and Aaron held out their hands to greet Susan.

"Nice to see you boys again," she said, placing her arms around them. "I'm sure you're both glad to have your parents back."

The boys smiled shyly, and nodded their heads.

The small group made their way around the ship, arriving at a beautiful outdoor lounge. Thomas and Susan were greeted along the way by several passengers.

"Who are all these people?" Susan asked.

"These were my colleagues for the last two and a half years," Alfred said.

"All these people worked with you in the bunker?"

Alfred nodded.

"Susan!"

Susan leapt from the couch. "Leila!"

"It's so great to see you again, Susan. My father especially asked me to make you feel at home."

Leila handed her a postcard.

"Your father?"

Thomas hugged Leila. "Leila is Raheem's daughter."

Susan's mouth dropped open. "Your father?"

"My father is alive and well."

"Raheem organised this cruise for those who had been prisoners in the bunker, and their family members," Thomas said.

Leila smiled, pointing to the card in Susan's hands. Susan read the card while a waiter served them drinks. On the front of the card was a picture of the Kansas prairie. The back of the card read, 'Dear Susan, your prairie is beautiful. See you soon'.

"My father will be with us tomorrow," Leila said.

Susan looked at Alfred and Kim holding each other. The card had rekindled a flame in her heart. She wiped a happy tear and turned to Thomas to change her train of thought.

"Thomas, tell us about the tunnel escape. It must have taken months to dig."

Thomas laughed. "We started working on the tunnel over three years ago."

"A masterpiece of engineering," Alfred said.

"But how did you know about the bunker?" Susan asked.

"Cruse abducted these guys." He pointed to the men around him.

"Giving him a complete monopoly of the latest battle technology," Alfred added.

"Raheem's son Hallej was working with Max Townsend. Max escaped to Russia, but Hallej was abducted and taken to the bunker." Thomas paused. "Here's Hallej now."

He waved to Ricky.

"Ricky is Raheem's son?" Susan asked.

"My young brother," Leila announced, smiling proudly.

"I'm still confused," Susan said.

"One of Scott's team, Greg Matthews, was unhappy with what was going on, so he sent the Flashlight list to the one person with enough resources to do something. Ricky's father."

Thomas looked at Leila.

"My father was already working on a plan to rescue Ricky, when he met you and Kim," Leila said. "He also sent the list to Alfred and several others, trying to warn them."

"I started saving copies of my work off site for protection. The flash drive that you found in Paris was a copy of my most valuable work," Alfred added.

"We covered Scott with tracking dust, much smaller than the human eye can detect. Most of the dust washed off, but we only needed one small speck to stick," Thomas said. "The night that Scott walked into the nightclub, an RFID scanner received the location data for everywhere he had been during the previous twelve months. We didn't need the location for every room in the bunker, just enough to navigate the main hallways and locate those being held captive."

"So, the whole event with my look-a-likes, was all about getting access to Scott?" Susan asked.

"That's right."

"Why did you stay hidden after the palace attack?" Susan asked, changing the topic.

"My father escaped the attack on the palace by hiding in the cinema. He used underground tunnels that led to the garden," Leila said. "He thought it was best that he and Thomas remain invisible and chose to work behind the scenes. Like a puppeteer."

"The dream about the puppet," Kim said.

Leila nodded.

"So, while Scott was chasing me like the gold ring, the real magic was happening in a different location," Susan said.

"When we realised that you wouldn't stop searching, we shadowed you for protection, and involved you in our plan to stop Cruse," Thomas said.

"You were following me the whole time?" Susan asked.

Thomas smiled. "The whole time. I believe you know Juan." He pointed to a man in an immaculate white suit approaching them.

"No way! Juan was working for you?"

Juan approached Susan and embraced her. "Great to see you again, Susan." He gave her a kiss on each cheek.

Thomas turned to Alfred and Kim. "What are your plans now?"

"We're not sure if we will stay in Florida, but Alfred wants to continue his research."

"I'm working on ways that nano technology can be used in space." He laughed. "No more Nano Dragons."

"Nano what?" Juan asked.

Kim punched Alfred on the shoulder in a display of playful affection.

"Please, no science lessons today," she said.

He smiled. "I'll save the lesson for another day."

"And what about you, Susan?" Thomas asked. "What are your plans?"

Susan thought for a moment. "Perhaps some more travel."

"Would Morocco be on the itinerary?" Kim asked, teasing.

"Somewhere peaceful, away from nano things."

Everyone laughed.

"Let me take you all to the upper deck," Thomas said. "We can watch the sunset."

The sunlight danced upon on the waves as the small group walked along the ship's deck and up a stairway. On the upper deck, they looked out across the bow, enjoying the beautiful ocean view.

"Sailing the Caribbean," Kim said, holding Alfred.

"How many more things on our bucketlist, Honey?" Alfred asked.

"Well, I've seen enough of Nevada to last a lifetime, so it's safe to say that won't be included."

Alfred laughed.

"This view reminds me of a quote my father taught me," Ricky said. "We must free ourselves of the hope that the sea will ever rest." He paused.

"We must learn to sail in high winds," Susan said.

THE END

About the Author

PETER SEWELL is an Australian author with a passion for travel, photography, and writing. His writing is inspired by his traveling adventures in more than 45 countries. He currently lives in Germany with his wife Annette. Along with writing, he also enjoys walking through the forest, hiking in the Italian Alps, or walking along the beach in Australia.

Peter is also an experienced personal coach and counsellor, who has helped hundreds of people overcome challenging situations and move forward to achieve their goals. His novels aim to offer encouragement and hope for those who are facing difficult situations in life. Along with personal coaching, Peter enjoys speaking to different groups on the topics of Faith, Leadership and Teamwork.

Acknowledgements

Special thanks to K.M. Weiland, Chandler Bolt, Joanna Penn and James Patterson, who showed me that publishing my novel was an achievable goal. Their expertise and encouragement were invaluable. My dear friends Joshua Buckle and Kerrie Gleeson were also a great source of inspiration, as I watched their writing journeys unfold. Thanks also to Emily Groves, Monique Manera, and Virginie Vin, who contributed their knowledge of the French language and locations within Paris. William Viquez was a great help with his cultural knowledge of Costa Rica. Daniel Huskisson for his technical knowledge on how to destroy a plane. Countless friends who offered ideas on how to dispose of dead bodies. (I didn't use their ideas, but they kept me entertained) Thanks also to the members of the Christian Writers Downunder group on Facebook, who were a wonderful support. Special thanks also to Kameel Magdali, who gave me the first signed copy of his first published book. That small action ignited a spark within me, and initiated my writing journey. Last but not least, my wife Annette, who has encouraged me every step.

To view a selection of Peter's
photography, or view excerpts from
his upcoming books, please visit:

www.petersewell.com